For Aunt Pat

Thank you Kim Liedberg for the cover photo.

Chapter 1

"Mary Elizabeth help yer Mama!" The tall elderly woman poked the shoulder of the younger one in front of her. "Imogene I do not need my daughters help or yours for that matter. I'm doin' jist fine on my own. You have insisted on treatin' me like I was twelve years old since I was...fourteen." scowled the stout woman leaning heavily on her cane.

"Eunice yer on a cane and some fairly steep concrete steps, it is not reassuring!" The woman snapped back.
"Oh for God sake lets not start this early in the morning." The younger woman tugged a hank of graying hair

away from her face and stared down the three old women she was accompanying.

"For two days now I've had to listen to the three of you prittle-prattle and bicker and I am just hoping we can get through one day peacefully!" She gave her Mother the stink eye and gently took her arm. Her Mother started to say something but Mary Elizabeth put up her hand.

"No more conversation!" She said firmly.

"I din't say a thing." Muttered Louise Branner as she hoisted herself up the steep stairs.

"You were about to." snipped Imogene.

"I was not." said Louise.

"Stop! Now! Or I'm goin' straight home and leavin' you three ladies on these stairs!"

The three elderly women had been friends forever and now as more and more time was behind them then before, they were still in it together.

"Look up there!" Imogene said stopping in her tracks and shielding her eyes, looked straight up.

"My goodness it's been a long time since I've taken a good long look at this place! It's kinda beautiful ain't it?" The four women took a long dreamy glance at the three story building in front of them. The long casement windows and red bricks stretched for as far as the eye could see. Well, these ladies eye's anyway. Each one was teeterin' just a tad over 80, their eyesight just wasn't what it once was.

For as long as anyone knew, this was the tallest building in town. The old building was imposing in it's simple grandeur. The ladies were staring up at the old Community High School, an institution all three attended in there youth and proudly graduated from.

    Until last year this building had been steadily used. Hundreds of graduating Seniors, cow licked freshmen, and everyone in between had spent time growing up and learning life in this building. But now there was a new place to learn. It was squat and one storied. Air conditioned and well lit. It had a catered cafeteria and served three meals a day to every kid that was hungry. In this old school you dragged a sack lunch with you day after day and prayed against ecol-I as the sacks sat in warm cloak-rooms hour after hour. Sometime in the 1950's they stuck a "lunch room" in the cold dank basement snugged up against the gym. You could get a hot lunch cooked right here on the premises for ten cents a day. Once they got Miss Ellie down there at the crack of predawn the food those kids ate couldn't be topped by much. She would crawl into that dark school at 4 AM and by the time the children arrived the whole place smelled of fresh baked light rolls and casserole.

    Miss Ellie would serve cobblers that would start fights in the parking lot, they were just that good.

  Now the old school was being 'retired'. It's long varnished hallways and tiny gymnasium were being put to rest under a wrecking ball. The whole town had turned out for speeches and free hot dogs the day the new school was dedicated. And there it sat, in the shadow of this grand edifice. Long and squat without distinction. These ladies had volunteered to go through the old classrooms and decide if there was anything worth saving. They were expected to be fair and unsentimental, a task best left to a much younger group.

"Well, I think we should go on up to the third floor today. No one has actually used that area for years on end. I think it's just basically been storage for as long as I've known." said Mary Catherine.

"Oh my! I remember the times we had up those stairs! Eunice exclaimed.

"I had my first cigarette up in that little bathroom up there. Remember that Imogene? You were with me." Eunice hung her head and chuckled right along with her lifelong friend.

"Of course I remember! I'm the one

that gave you the smoke in the first place." Imogene slapped her thigh.

"You took one puff, turned green and fell right in that leaky old bathroom sink up there!" All four women smiled and stared up, shading there crinkled faces from the baking September sun. There eyes grazed the top floor of the old school.

"Well, best get a move on then huh?" said Louise looping her hand through Eunice's arm and squeezing.

"Times a wastin' ain't it. And Lord knows we ain't got all that much left!"

Chapter 2

"How on a stack a seven bibles are we gonna git Eunice up them stairs!" asked Imogene gazing up at the winding staircases. Each set of stairs had a landing with a huge curved window facing what was once a beautiful expanse of lawn rolling elegantly to the curb. These days it was just a mess of mud turned dirt from the construction of the new building.

"Don't you worry your old ass about me Imogene Elliot. I can git myself anywhere without the help a you or my beautiful daughter!" Mary Catherine rolled her eyes and started up taking each step carefully and holding her Mama's hand. It was a slow process but Mary Catherine knew she had to be watchful. Her Mother wouldn't say a word even if she was hurtin', not with this crowd anyway.

As they approached the first landing, a fan shaped window taller then they were caught there attention. They all stopped and rested their arms on the worn and pitted brass bar that saved many a child from a horrible death bustin' thru while takin' a miscalculated turn. They all breathed heavily and and took a long look.

Mary Catherine saw a mess of dumpsters and concrete blocks where as the elderly women all smiled slightly remembering the days long ago standing in this very spot watching for friends or discussing boys. Mary Catherine touched her Mama's shoulder and let her catch her breath as the memories flooded back.

"Oh girls....didn't we have fun." Eunice sighed. "Oh you bet we did!" Louise replied touching her hand to Eunice's.

"It wasn't all fun and games now was it girls? We had our share a hard times as well around here din't we?" Imogene piped in. Eunice shook her head.

"You have always been such a little ray a sunshine Imogene! I swan...I don't know how we have put up with you all these years." Imogene smiled.

"Y'all love me I guess." she pouted.

Slowly they made there way to the place where the handrail finally came to an end. The halls looked just a little darker up here, just a little less spacious.

"Is it smaller up here?" asked Mary Catherine.

"It is Honey. I'll show you when we git to the outside again. It's a little bit indented up here on the top. Seems different don't it? I always liked it up here. Didn't seem like the rest of the school somehow." said Louise.

"Good place to sneak up and take a breather for yourself durin' a rough school day."

"Lookie down that way!" shouted Imogene. "That was Mr Snow's homeroom. I started every single day of my high school life right there in that very room." She reminisced.

"Come on girls lets go take a look." Off they toddled with Eunice bringing up the rear none the less enthusiastic. They pushed the heavy door open and gazed in at the empty classroom. This was one of the very few rooms decked out with risers so the desks sat slightly raised from one another as you went further back in the small room. The desks were gone now, sold to a salvage company in Tulsa that loaded up everything they wanted and left the place naked of much of it's charm. Mary Catherine knew that somewhere, somehow, someone was buying a desk with her Mama's name carved in it with a declaration of eternal love for some boy or the next, certainly not her Daddy. The blackboards that ran the entire front of the room were actually black, and still held the powder of year after year of math problems and run on sentences.

"Oh look y'all!" Mary Catherine heard from the hallway. Louise was standing at an open doorway with a huge grin plastered across her face.

"It's the infamous third floor girls bathroom!" She said proudly. Mary Catherine stuck her head in the door to two small stalls a single sink and a gigantic radiator that took up most of one wall. Everything was coated with dust and dirt and looked far from salvageable.

"Looks like Cowboys used this bathroom!" exclaimed Mary Catherine. "Or miners, maybe roughnecks."

"I don't remember ever being up here in all my high school days." She ran her hand over the beaded board doors of the tiny stalls. "It's so much different then the rest of the school isn't it?" She asked looking into the faces of the older women.

"Yes child, it is!" Piped up Eunice. "I think this floor is much more like the original school then the rest. By the time you were here Honey they had this all shut down. It got lost in the renovatin' shuffle I guess." Eunice shoot her head.

"Sure brings back memories to codgers our age tho!" She gave a wistful grin and turned to the others.

"Come on ladies, lets git to some of those boxes and crates and see if there's anything the wrecking ball needs to avoid up here..shouldn't take long. It is a little bit sparse up here ain't it." She helped the ladies get there bearings and wrangled them down to the other end of the long center hallway. Mary Catherine pulled a few crates over for the ladies to sit on and they got started.

"Oh my goodness! Will you take a look at this! Eunice exclaimed as she pulled a stack of playbills from 1942 out of a crate. "Oh I knew so many of the people in this play...Romeo And Juliet. This was just a few years before my time but look at those faces will ya." Eunice slowly leafed through the thin magazine 'tut tuting' from time to time.

"Mama! Take a look around you. We have a world of things to go through and your stuck on the first thing you put yer hands on? We simply don't have the time!" Mary Catherine took the playbills out of the elder woman's hand and scooted the crate out of her reach.

"That looks like a pile of stuff from the theater department, no need to keep any of that. If anyone had wanted this stuff they would have gotten it long ago, besides, most of them are dead!" she said just a little harshly to her Mother.

"What about all these old bunson burners and test tubes and....ewww! God only knows whats in those containers! You think we need to keep all that Girls?" said Imogene.

"No, Honey I think they got all sort a new things like that in that shiny new building and Lord only knows what kind a disease has been captured for posterity in those old petrie dishes." Louise waved her hand at the group.

"We may want to make mention a those for some sort of bio-hazard disposal tho." Louise rubbed her dusty forehead. "Oh my, do you girls remember when Osage Lewis mixed up some sort of concoction right over there in the third floor science lab back in the day? Why, they had to close the school for three days or so!" Imogene laughed and slapped her knee.

"Lordy I remember all that! People were pukin' up right in the hallways! What a sight! Eunice narrowed her eyes. "I was one of those folks gettin' sick from here to there." Eunice rolled her eyes.

"Y'all can laugh all you want but I've never been sicker in my life!" The three elderly woman tut tutted for a second and went right back to sorting.

Mary Catherine dragged another large old steamer trunk out of the shadows and placed it in front of Imogene. "There you go. Now we're makin' a little progress." She laid her hand on the woman's thin shoulder and sat back down on her own milk crate. She was leafing thru a moldering pile of old P.E. Uniforms when she noticed Imogene had stopped diggin' thru her crate.

"Imogene? You okay?" All three ladies glanced up at there dear friend.

"You ain't havin' a heart attack or a stroke or anything are you? Imogene?

You look all washed out." said Eunice. As the old woman turned toward her friends a tear spilled down her wrinkled cheek. The woman all leaned forward and gazed down into the trunk in front of their friend. Louise gasped and put her hand to her mouth.

"Lord have mercy!" exclaimed Eunice. "Well, if that ain't Clyde Ray Tummel. That's where he disappeared to." They all sadly looked down at the mummified remains of a teen-aged boy laying peacefully in the crate. He was wearing a Varsity Jacket with "52" embroidered on a basketball across his left breast. His blue jeans were pegged and his blonde hair hung sweetly over his forehead.

"He was always such a pretty boy wasn't he?" said Louise. Mary Catherine stood abruptly.

"We need to call the police!" she practically shouted.

"No....I think we need to call Casey." said Imogene.

Chapter 3

Casey was tearin' down the highway travelin' to Tulsa. She had the music up loud and no one was rulin' the roadway like she was on this bright September day.

It was a sad, sad moment when her beloved little Toyota truck died a horrible death. It had been a cold day the previous February when white steam and water blew out of Toy Terrific's old engine. After 466,000 miles that little pick up had done it's part..and more. This new/old Chevy truck was a pretty blue bucket a fun!

For all the many years Casey and her Toy Terrific had traveled together she had never had music. Casey was so enjoying not only having a radio that actually worked but a CD player as well. So she cranked it high and flew down the back roads and highways of Oklahoma in what she thought was perfect style.

Today she was in particularly good spirits, she was on the way to the Tulsa Airport to pick up her good friend Benj who was jettin' in for vacation. Two weeks with Benj and Casey's heart was flyin' just as fast as her truck.

As she pulled into the arrivals area the only person standing there was one she knew well.

"Can I give you a ride little girl?" Casey said rollin' down the electric window and grinnin' to beat the band.

"Well, well...just look at this thing!" exclaimed Benj. "It's a real truck! No more tiny little putt putt pretending to be an Oklahoma driver, nope..this is a real honest to God truck!" Benj laughed and patted the metallic side of the dark blue Chevy Truck.

"Now stop tryin' to look all cool and get your ass out here and hug me before I evaporate in this heat! I'm not used to it anymore you know!" Casey was happy to oblige.

Benj had been Casey's friend and runnin' partner for over twenty years. Not long before she had joined Casey on her farm for what was supposed to be a workin' summer. A couple of years later and Benj was almost talkin with the sweet little twang Oklahoman's easily sported. Casey missed her friend terribly, but jobs were scarce out here in the middle of nowhere and before Casey knew it, Benj had transplanted herself back among the hustle and bustle of city life. But here she was back again if only for a week or two, Casey was beside herself.

Benj settled in the soft buttery leather seat next to her friend. She wiggled her butt around and gave a fast grin to Casey

"Stylin' here sister! Nice ride! Well, we can't just go home! We need to go have some fun somewhere don't you think?" Benj flashed a sideways grin Casey's way.

"Benj I don't have....."

"Stop! Just shut up and drive will ya. I've got cash. Lets hit the Casino for the buffet lunch and toss a little change around. Whataya think Case? Drive on over to the Hard Rock and lets live a little huh?" Casey smiled to herself. It was a money issue that took Benj out of her little farm life in the first place. She was glad her friend was doing well, and besides, the buffet was delicious and Casey couldn't remember the last time she ate in a restaurant. This promised to be a wonderful day.

Chapter 4

"So, what's been happin' in the big town Case?" Benj sat back in her chair and splayed her feet out in front of her. The buffet was indeed as good as advertised and the two women sat pokin' straws in tall, icy refill glasses of Dr Pepper. Casey spun her straw and smiled at Benj.

"What exactly do you mean? Am I being haunted? Is ectoplasm drippin' down the walls of my house? No Benj! All is well. All is back to tiny and boring in my life and I'm so happy to have it that way!" Casey took a long swig off her Dr Pepper and glanced smugly at her friend.

"No wraith's hidin' in the rafters. No lost souls hangin' in the barns. I am happily alone out here now." Benj gave her friend a sideways glance.

"Yeah Buddy, you thought that before." Casey shuffled her feet and stared into her glass.

"You know, I'm glad I could help with all that out at Lawnwood School it's true. But, truth is I don't want to do it again. I just want to have my farm and my old folks and live happily ever after. That's dandy with me." A smilin' waitress wandered by.

"Y'all need a refill on those Dr Peppers Honey?" Casey pointed at hers and said.

"Make it diet please." The girl zipped away and Casey looked up and grinned at her friend.

"So, What's up with wantin' to throw a little cash around? You still willin'? Let's suck down these drinks and get to it then!" Casey kicked her friend under the table.

"Let's go Girly Girl! Put your money where your mouth is!" Benj flicked a straw wrapper at Casey and took a long pull off her cold drink.

"Let's go then"...and off they went.

As the big truck rumbled down the highway finding it's way toward home, Benj tossed an angry look in Casey's direction.

"You know there's something wrong with you." Benj said goading Casey.

"Oh stop! For the love a God! It wasn't my fault and you know it!" Casey gripped the steering wheel harder and tried her best to look angry.

"I was winnin'! I was winnin' big! Then you had to come along and touch my machine, just touch it and boom! All that winnin' was over in a psychic flash! You know you have some weird touchin' affliction." Casey rolled her eyes and started to laugh in spite of herself.

"If that's all it takes to get your winnin' streak to roar to an end then yes, I am responsible!" Casey waved her hands over her head like she was at a revival meeting.

"Cut that out! Put your hands back on the steering wheel! Your gonna wreck us!" shouted Benj. Both women laughed to beat the band. Enjoying each others company was always an easy task for these two. They fell into a never ending conversation as they zoomed down the highway. So many things had happened since Benj had left. Folks had died or left or changed partners. All the goin's on of a small town passed between them as Benj tried to catch up. Before they knew it the loud "Bringgg!" of Casey's phone interrupted the girls trip down memory lane. Benj grabbed it off the dash and said.

"It's Miss Imogene". Benj whispered.

"Why you whisperin'? Answer it!" Nodded Casey.

Chapter 5

"Hello." Casey smiled to herself as she listened to Benj.

"No, Miss Imogene, this isn't Casey. It's Benj! Do you remember me?" No, I'm not back for good. Just a little vacation I'm afraid. I just flew into Tulsa and Casey and I had a bite a lunch before we headed home. No Ma'am we went to the Hard Rock. No Ma'am I think you'd all enjoy it the buffet is wonderful. No, Ma'am it's not to pricey." Benj rolled her eyes at Casey and smiled. Benj always got a kick out of 'Casey's Elderly Folk' as she refereed to them. Casey was a Home Health Worker and she cared for several elderly people at any given time. Miss Imogene had been her client for years.

"Oh I'm doing well Ma'am and how are you these days?" Benj chattered.

"No, I'm afraid I can't move back to town Miss Imogene I have a good job in the city now. Yes Ma'am. Yes Ma'am. I know the city is a dangerous place. Yes Ma'am, I am very careful about myself. Oh, I'm sure we could swing by the old High School before we go home today. What are y'all doing up there anyway? Okay, I guess I'll just have to find out when we get there. We're comin' thru Calvin now so it won't be long. Alright then. See ya soon. Good to talk to you as well."

"What was that all about?" asked Casey.

"No idea. I could hear Mary Elizabeth in the background, she sounded kinda exasperated so heaven only knows." Benj settled herself down into the seat and and closed her eyes.

"Smells like Oklahoma." she mused.

"Mary Elizabeth is always exasperated when it comes to her Mama, I wonder what's up." Casey sniffed the air.

"Smells like dust to me Kiddo."

"Same thing." grinned Benj.

Casey pulled the big truck into the circle drive surrounding the old High School. Her and Benj shrugged there shoulders at one another as they eyed the old bricks.

"This was a nice building. Lots of kids got some sort of education here." Casey mused as she made her way to the front doors.

"Well, that's for sure but it's seen a better day. Time for this town to tip toe into the future don't you agree?"

Benj asked as they swung open the heavy brass doors.

"No." replied Casey. "Miss Ellie worked in this place for so many years you could barely count 'em. I hate to ever see a fine old historical place like this get raised. It's a crime if you ask me. Yoohoo!" She shouted as they entered the main hallway.

"Why did you yoohoo?" said Benj shaking her head. "No one under the age of ninety yoohoo's. People our age just call out..."Hey! Where are y'all?" Benj shouted.

"Well, thank you Benj for schoolin' me on the proper use of the language. I'm sure it will come in very handy in my future life." Casey scoffed and gave her friend a sideways look. Somewhere from above they heard a faint,

"Yoohoo! Up here girls!" Casey

coughed lightly and raised an eyebrow at Benj as they started there assent.

"Man this is really a lovely old building isn't it?" Casey ran her hands over the shining wooden railings complete with brass fittings. "I'll bet you won't find an ounce of brass in that new cracker box they call a school house." Casey exclaimed.

"It smells like school." moped Benj. Casey smiled to herself, she was thinking the very same thing.

"Up here girls! All the way up to the third floor." Miss Louise hollered down the staircase.

As they turned into the dark upper hallway they could see the ladies gathered around several old trunks and boxes at the end of the hall. The afternoon sunlight was streaming in turning dust particles into tiny jewels fluttering through the afternoon air.

"Come on now! Come on!" Hustled Miss Louise as she met them halfway. "Were so sorry to have to interrupt your vacation Benj, so good to see you Honey!" Miss Louise grabbed Benj's hand and held it tightly. Casey lagged behind taking in the glory of the fine old structure as Miss Louise dragged Benj toward the others. Casey was used to people flocking around Benj. She normally just sat back and smiled. Benj had a charming way to her that attracted everyone. Casey lifted an eyebrow as Miss Louise dragged a giggling Benj around an ancient trunk standing open at the end of the hallway. Benj was chatting away and greeting the other ladies with hugs . As she turned and glanced into the truck she shouted

"Oh Shit!" and stepped back almost

tripping over two or three crates laid out around them.

"Casey No!" she shouted regaining her footing but it was to late. Casey, looking confused, reached out and grabbed the corner of the trunk.

"Oh shit! Here we go again!" Benj cried trying to catch Casey as she slumped to the floor.

The heat was the first thing she noticed. It was a hot and humid day. The bees were buzzing everywhere as she saw two boys laying half naked by a fast running little stream. The landscape looked oddly familiar but her eyes were drawn to the boys. They were stripped to there skivvy's and obviously enjoying the quiet day by the creek.

Casey watched as they poked and laughed and teased one another. They couldn't have been more then sixteen or so. There hair was long and matted like it had been awhile since a comb or brush had passed through much less a pair of shears.

They were sweet in a puppy-like way and Casey found herself smiling at there antics. They reminded Casey of the FFA kids she used to have come help out on her little farm. They laughed and shoved each other like teenage boys have done forever. Casey shook her head as they splashed into the stream yelling and hooting to beat the band.

Then from somewhere in the distance came a sharp pop! Both boys sat up quickly and scrambled for pants and blouses. Several more Pops cut the air around them as they dragged gray caps onto there heads and started running bent in half and keeping low.

They looked so young and scared, helpless and confused as they scurried along the happy little creek. Another volley of Pops and one of the boys fell to the ground. He was small and blond and a little delicate. Casey could see a stream of darkness coming from under his cap. The other boy pulled and tugged and cried for his friend but he was also small and the next volley removed his jaw.

The boy jerked up crying a horrible cry then fell quiet next to his buddy.

"Casey! Casey! You okay? Come on now Case. Shit! Casey!" Benj fanned her friend and held her head in her lap. "Your okay, your fine. You've just been visitin' another dimension again is all." Casey stirred slightly and opened her eyes. Around her in the gathering darkness all she saw were worried eyes.

"Hi Benj." Casey said looking up into the concerned face of her long time friend. Benj rolled her eyes and put her hand on Casey's warm head.

"Hi Casey. Ready to go home now?" She said softly pushing dust off her friends face.

"Yeah I am!...What the hell is in that trunk anyway?" Casey said pulling herself up.

"Some dead kid." said Benj.

Chapter 6

Benj and Casey sat cross legged against a bank of lockers that lined the hallway of the third floor. They watched as Sheriff Elwood Pincher shook his head slowly over the crate.

"Man, I remember when this boy went missin'. I was just a kid at the time but the whole town was up in arms." He glanced at the people lining the room. "And here he laid the whole damn time. Right here big as life, or somethin'." The Sheriff shook his head again and motioned to Danny from the Funeral Home to go ahead.

"Dang!" Elwood muttered under his breath as they slowly started moving the boys body. His eyes rolled toward Benj and Casey.

"What are you two doin' here anyways? Good Lord Miss Casey, why are you always around when there's a body or two layin' about?" The Sheriff narrowed his eyes at the girls.

"We called them!" Piped up Miss Evelyn. "Elwood you know Casey knows things! We wanted to know if Casey could figure this out before we called on you! No disrespect Son, but you gotta know how Casey is!"

Elwood sighed heavily.

"Aunt Evelyn you should have called me first, you know that! You know I'm the law in this town now. Sometimes I think you forget that. Like those parking tickets and those tires stacked up in yer yard. You know I'm gonna come out there and ticket you for all that mess!" Elwood turned to Casey.

"Casey you know anything? You figure anything out when you were passed out on the floor over there?" He muttered.

"No Sheriff I don't know a damn thing." sighed Casey. Miss Imogene almost fell over herself jumping up.

"Casey fell into one of her fits Elwood! Right here on this dusty floor! She dropped just like a steer to slaughter! I know she seen somethin'! That was clear as ice!" Miss Imogene pointed and waved her hand over her head like a crazy woman. "What did you see Casey?"

Casey looked up slowly. "I honestly have no idea Miss Imogene. I'm gonna have to mull this over a bit and get back to you on that." Casey reached over and took her friends hand.

"Help me up will ya Benj?" Casey started to rise and Benj pushed her back to the ground.

"Honest to God Case, I think you should just sit there and breath for a few minutes. You skidded over right on your bean." Casey looked confused as she lightly tapped the sore spot on her forehead.

"Stop that!, it hurts!" She glanced up at Benj.

"Yeah, I think you might have a hefty bruise right there, maybe even a shiner." Benj reached toward Casey's head and had her hand swatted away.

"I'm tellin' you, this sort of thing has got to stop! I can't just be fallin' over willy nilly. Who's the dead kid in the box anyway?" Casey stuck a finger toward the trunk.

"Clyde Ray Tummel." replied Miss Louise. Casey looked confused.

"Who's Clyde Ray Tummel?" She

asked.

"Oh, he was the sweetest boy!" Answered Miss Louise.

"Louise was always a little sweet on him." Imogene clucked rolling her eyes.

"Hold on! Hold on!" shouted Casey. "You mean you ladies know this mummified kid in this trunk? I mean you knew him back in the day, when he was breathin' and all?" Casey stared hard at the elderly women.

"Well, Of course!" Explained Imogene. "We went to school with him, he was our classmate."

"Oh sweet Jesus!" sighed Casey. "Not again. I need to stay out of schoolhouses!" Casey's thought's drifted back to her adventures at the long abandoned Lawnwood School.

All three women looked at Casey

shock in there old eyes.

"Casey we would appreciate it if you wouldn't use the Lords name in vain around us! I know you younger folk don't take mind, but we do. " Tutted Evelyn.

Chapter 7

A couple years earlier Casey had been involved in solving a long standing serial murder that took place at the ruins of Lawnwood, another local school. As much as she wanted to push all that under the closest rug, Casey's name had become a household one in the surrounding area. Her ability to interact with folks no longer among the living was a skill everyone whispered about.

"Hey you wanna stop in at the Dairy Queen for one of those big burgers? You hungry? This big truck drives really nice! I'm gonna have to make use of this while I'm here!" Benj rounded the corner into town and figured Casey wouldn't want to cook anything that evening, and honestly either did she.

"You buyin'?" asked Casey leaning her head against the cool window glass.

"Yep!" Answered Benj swingin' the big truck into the parking area of the local 'hot spot'. "You want a Blizzard or a Dilly Bar or anything like that? May as well. Actually I should just pick up a box of Dillie's while we're here, then we'll just have 'em. What a ya' think Case?" Benj touched her friends shoulder and watched worriedly for a reaction.

"Benj I'm fine. You know this sort of thing just knocks the snot right outta me." Casey smiled weakly at Benj. "Don't worry. You know as well as I do I'll feel fine come morning.

Sometimes I wonder if this sort of thing takes a little snip of life out of me every time it happens though. You know what I mean? Like the little times I spend in Lalaland are all cumulative toward the end of my life. Sure do knock the livin' daylights outta me that's for sure!" Casey laid her head back against the cool glass.

"Yeah, get some Dilly Bars, that sounds really good. We can put 'em in the freezer."

The evening was warm and balmy as the Oklahoma sun finally dipped below the western treeline. The sky was painted with the brilliant oranges and blues that told the world it wasn't gonna give up easy. A fight was on that the sun would never win, but still would rise tomorrow to try the struggle yet one more time.

"You comfy?" asked Benj as she

threw an old quilt over Casey's feet.

"Feelin' any better? Move will ya?" Benj scooted Casey's legs further up on the sofa and dropped heavily beside her. Casey smiled and curled up a little more allowing her friend a bit more room.

"I'm feeling just fine. I'm glad to have you here. I've missed you Benj. The place isn't the same without you." Benj looked away.

"Yeah, yeah, yeah! I noticed the grass is to long and the fences need a little shorin' up. Your lettin' the place go to seed Casey!" Benj slapped Casey's leg and grinned at her.

"I know you miss me. I miss you..and the animals, and this run down little hole in the wall you call home. I just can't make a living here Casey, you know that. And....I have to admit hot and cold running water and

McDonald's on every corner and actually going to a store to buy something has become a way of life for me now...it's not a luxury anymore. I kinda like the city life again Case, not gonna lie." Casey snugged up a little tighter in her quilt.

"Yeah I know."

"You gonna tell me what you saw today out there in the Twilight Zone? Or, are you gonna keep it to yourself where it's gonna fester and spread and turn into some terrible brain conquering nastiness? Casey threw back her head and chuckled.

"Not sure it's all that consuming Benjy my dear! Actually I don't have a clue what it was all about. It was just two boys messin' around in a creek, havin' a blast when somebody started taken' potshots at 'em, laid 'em out cold dead. Nothin' to do with Clyde what's his name in the box!" Casey looked at Benj in the growing darkness.

"Funny thing is they looked like baby soldiers. Like drummer boys or buglers. They weren't old enough to be regular enlisted guys." Casey watched Benj's face.

"Benj.....they looked like Confederate boys. Does that make any sense at all?" Benj looked down. Casey could no longer see her face in the dark room.

"Not to me it doesn't. But it could...to someone." Benj quietly replied.

Chapter 8

As morning meandered across the Canadian River Valley, Benj woke to the smell of the best coffee in all of Hughes County.

"Hey!" She shouted. "You already up and poppin'?" Casey grinned down into the potatoes she was slicin'.

"Better get your ass up and out to the hen house If your expectin' fresh eggs with this breakfast!" Casey shouted in return. Then she heard the soft padding of slippered feet headin' for the bathroom and knew her threat wasn't taken lightly.

"I'm the guest. I shouldn't have to gather the damn eggs!" Casey heard the toilet flush and the sink faucet turn on.

"Oh guest my ass! You want eggs you go get 'em!" The screen door slammed and Casey knew the day was off and running. She had taken a few days off to spend some time with Benj on her vacation but not many. Money was always tight but life was meant to be enjoyed...and she was gonna do it!

She could hear Benj in the barnyard talking to the sheep and the dogs and the ever present barn cat, Jack. She pulled the curtain back and watched as Benj ran a few feet with the whole bunch running with her. Then she'd stop on a dime and laugh as the dogs kept running. Benj was breathing hard as she tumbled into the kitchen slamming the door and carefully placing the freshest eggs on earth on the table.

"Six eggs! Not bad huh?" Casey

couldn't help but smile.

"Little outta shape there kiddo? Get a little winded gatherin' eggs?" Casey teased.

"I think Karen is gonna start settin'. She was pretty protective of that egg!" Benj pointed at a big beautiful brown orb she had just brought in.

"She almost pecked me!"

"That's cause she doesn't remember you anymore. She doesn't peck at me!" Casey teased.

"She remembers me! Damn, I haven't been gone all that long! Benj complained.

"She's a chicken Benj. I'm not sure she can carry a memory all the way down memory lane." Casey laughed.

The animals on this farm were coddled and cared for from the second they arrived or were born. No one was mean or spiteful in the least.

They were all like big pets, or small pets, as the case may be. Benj finally got a good look at her good buddy this morning. The afternoons escapades had taken a toll for sure.

Casey was smiling and obviously happy on this sunny morning but her face told another story. There were deep, dark smudges under her navy blue eyes and her face looked just a tiny bit older somehow. Benj wondered if Casey had been right about these spells taking just a tiny bit of life out of her.

"Hey'd somebody just pull in?" Casey turned toward the front door her hands covered in flour. "Go check Benj!" Before she could get there, the doorway was filled with the formidable figure of Sheriff Elwood Pitcher, holding his hat in his hand and just about to knock.

"Knew you was home when I seen yer truck Casey, so I thought I'd stop in." The big man said. "Ya got anymore a that good smellin' coffee you could share with a thirsty man?"

Casey broke a couple more eggs in the fry pan as she sat a big cup of hot coffee in front of the Sheriff. "Sit down Elwood, how do you like your eggs?" Casey asked. The Sheriff took a big swill of coffee.

"Over hard if you don't mind Miss Casey, thank you. I don't care for any of that slimy stuff." Benj plopped down across from the man and stirred a dollop of sugar into her cup.

"Any news about the dead boy in the box Sheriff?" She asked.

"Well, ain't no big news that the kid was missin'. That's been a story since I was a child." He took another heavy swill of coffee. "Mighty good Miss Casey, mighty good! Everybody just thought he run off with some drummer girl or with the circus back then ya know." Casey and Benj looked at each other.

"Oh that was a thing back then! Boy's runnin' off with the circus. Oh yeah! It was common in these parts, or beatniks." Benj looked up from her coffee with a look of shock on her face.

"Beatniks?" She asked.

"Oh yeah, folks had a fear of beatniks back then. Anybody different got the goin' over ya know." Elwood eyed the plate of bacon with lust written all over his sunburned face. Casey put the platter of bacon and eggs in front of both of her guests.

"He was a wild kid that Clyde Ray was. Nobody dreamed he met an end like he did. Boy never left the schoolhouse I'd reckon. Pass the salt there Benj will ya?"

Casey pulled a pan of hot biscuits from the oven and dumped them in a napkin lined basket. She set the basket on the table in front of both sets of wide eyes.

"Lord have mercy!" muttered the Sheriff as he helped himself to a couple of fat cats-head biscuits and some homemade blackberry jam.

"How'd he get in the trunk?" asked Benj.

"No livin' idea." nodded Elwood. "We're gonna send that trunk off to Oklahoma City and have those forensics folks take a gander at it for awhile. See if they can come up with anything. We ain't in no hurry tho. Kid's been moulderin' there a long time, no reason to get huffy now." Everyone nodded.

"Tell you what tho Casey, those ole' ladies are swearin' on the bible you seen somethin' while keeled over up there on the third floor. Anything you wanna tell me?" Casey plopped down at the head of the table and started nibblin' at a biscuit.

"No Sheriff, I saw a couple kids messin' around in a creek then getting shot dead is all I saw. Nothin' to do with Clyde Ray at all. I'm as confused as you are." The Sheriff wiped his mouth on a napkin and stood.

"Well, if you figure anything out let me know. I'm not sure how that hoodoo voodoo that you do works but well, I seen it work before so I'm not gonna discount that. I am gonna try to smooth the feathers on those ole' hens in town before they bust an artery or somethin'. My Aunt Evelyn is the worst of 'em. Thank you for the breakfast. That was the best I've had in a long time I'll tell ya what, my wife hit sixty and decided she wasn't gonna cook no more." He shook his head sadly and walked toward the door. Casey grinned.

"Anytime Sheriff." Elwood turned. "Oh Honey don't say that! I'll be back in that chair tomorrow! Y'all have a good day now."

Chapter 9

"What a wonderful day!" Casey tossed a glance at Benj. "Thank you my friend. It was exactly what the doctor ordered." Benj rocked back in her favorite porch chair.

"You are sincerely welcome Ma'am! It was fun wasn't it? It's been a long, long time since we just cruised around the countryside taken in the sites and breathin' easy. I just loved it. Thank you! And you didn't do one crazy, weird thing all day. Didn't strike up a conversation with any dearly departed at all." Both women laughed into the quiet night.

"I try hard to keep my association with the 'not so living' to a minimum you know." Casey joked.

"Well Case the fallin' over in a faint is sort of a dead giveaway, to coin a phrase. None to subtle." Benj glanced at Casey in the failing light.

"Yeah, I wish I could curb that part." They both stared peacefully into the velvety darkness.

"Not many bugs out here tonight. What's that all about? Isn't it just thick with nasty flying, crawlin' things by this time of year?" Benj wondered.

"Had a little cold snap, they'll be back." Casey closed her eyes and listened to the bullfrogs down at the pond.

"They always are. Hey will you make me some of that cucumber salad I like so much tomorrow?" Asked Benj.

"O' course I will. The kind with the sour cream and vinegar? Yeah I can make that. Gotta pick up some green onions on the way home is all. I think I'm gonna go tuck myself in bed. It was such a nice day. Thank you for lunch. Boy I'll tell you what, I just can't even remember the last time I ate in a restaurant." Mused Casey. Benj rolled her eyes.

"I swear if you don't stop thanking me I'm never takin' you anywhere again! Enough!" Casey smiled.

"Fine, Goodnight! You comin' in?"
"Na, Gonna sit out here and smoke a cigarette." Benj waited.....

"I can't even believe your still smoking! What are you the last person that smokes in Chicago now? Geeze Benj, I can't even believe it! I'm going to bed. Enjoy your smoke!" Casey turned on her heel and walked in the house. Benj grinned as she pulled a cigarette from her bag and lit it.

Benj's eyelashes fluttered. Something jarred her from her deep, quiet sleep. There was nothing more comfortable then this hundred year old bedstead in this rundown old farmhouse. Benj closed her eyes and settled herself back in for a fine sleep.

"No!" There it was again. It was coming from Casey's room. Benj jumped out of bed and walked carefully toward Casey's open bedroom door.

"Case?" She asked poking her head around the corner. "You okay?" Casey was sitting bolt upright in her bed. She was staring toward the corner of her darkened room. Benj blinked herself just a little more awake. Casey looked pissed as hell sitting there in her nighty.

"Case?" Benj asked again.

"Benj?" Case said slowly. "I'm not

gonna have it!" Casey gritted her teeth her eyes never wavering from the corner of the room. "I won't have these damn spooks coming into my home! I'm not gonna put up with this shit." Casey's eyes filled with tears. "This is my area! This is my home Benj!" Benj walked into the room trying hard to see what Casey was seeing. She reached out and grabbed Casey as she slumped over in her arms.

The birds were still chirping and the sun was shining brightly as Casey looked around the familiar scene. She looked to where the two boys had fallen in what seemed only moments before. The bodies were gone but the crushed grass and ground were stained with blood. Somewhere on the wind Casey heard cries of pain and gunfire. She wanted to run. She wanted to drop in the tall grass and hide. Suddenly she realized the air smelled of gunpowder and smoke. She glanced at the little bubbling creek just below her and saw streaks of red running through the cool clear water.

"Casey! Casey! Come back! Casey what the hell is goin' on?" The words seemed so far away. It was Benj. She wanted to be there, with Benj..in her cozy little bedroom not here, not in this horror.

"Casey! Damn it Case! Come on! Come on back. Don't cry, come back!" She felt Benj's hand on her face and hot tears streaking her cheeks. She could almost see Benj, her face worried and fearful. An explosion shook the ground she was standing on, men cried out in sorrow.

"Benj! Casey grabbed hard to Benj's neck and held on tightly. "Save me Benj! They're shooting!" Casey cried.

"I'm here, your fine, your fine." Benj held tight to her trembling friend. "Case? You with me now? You here?" Casey lifted her head slowly wiping her face on Benj's sleeve.

"Yeah. I'm here. Shit fire Man, this sucks!"

Chapter 10

"Well, If you want my opinion you shouldn't even attempt to go to work today." Benj said pouring Casey a fresh cup of coffee. "You look like hell on a stick." Benj added. Casey rolled her eyes in Benj's direction.

"I kinda feel like hell on a stick but I really have to go to work, for many reasons." sighed Casey.

"Name six." said Benj. Casey sat back in her chair and took a sip of her coffee. Her face scrunched and she glanced at Benj. "Yeah, yeah, yeah I don't make coffee as good as you do! Shoot me." A small smile crossed over Casey.

"No, I'm not gonna shoot anyone." She look shyly at Benj. "I do appreciate the coffee and damn am I glad your here right now! I know it's not the perfect country vacation but I'd be hard pressed without you!

"I know, I'm a miracle in the making...name six please." Casey shut her eyes. I need to take care of my elderly, they depend on me." Casey poked up a finger.

"There's one." counted Benj.

"Cut it out Benj." Casey flashed a rare look of real anger toward her dear friend. "I am very tired and just a little upset. I've got a specter looming' about in my bedroom now, not a reassuring situation." She glared. "I think the sooner I get to the bottom of all this the better." Casey turned and was about to walk out the door.

"Benj!" She hollered before exiting. "Thank you. I know you only want the best for me. I'll see you tonight. I think we have a date with some cucumber salad don't we?" Casey grinned as she bounded out the door.

A look of concern passed over Benj's face. She leaned back almost dangerously in the old vinyl and chrome kitchen chair and sipped her coffee. She squished her face. "Damn! I really don't make coffee as well as Case!" She exclaimed to herself.

Benj mused and sipped and sipped and mused till the morning was well along and the Oklahoma sun was high in the giant sky. Suddenly Benj tipped her chair back to it's rightful position and abruptly stood up. She plopped her coffee cup in the sink and ran a stream of water into it.

"I'll go visit Miss Constance!" She said slamming' herself out the front door!

Chapter 11

The imposing stone library enveloped Benj like a comfy old sweater. The musty smell of ancient books long untouched and unnoticed tweaked her nose like an long lost friend. Benj just had to smile as she ran her hand over the brass railing leading to the front desk.

"Now Honey you jus cain't take out another movie till you bring back the other's you have. You know that Brenda June!" Miss Constance was waggin' a finger and scolding a woman with a tiny baby braced on her hip. Benj slipped by without a ripple. She wanted to take a look around before she faced her good buddy Miss Constance.

The Library looked the same, maybe a little rougher then Benj remembered, but the same over all. The front was a hub of activity since it doubled as a free video rental. Miss Constance tried hard to keep an inventory of recent movies on hand but mostly spent money from her own pocket doing so.

There wasn't much to keep folks occupied in this town so the video library was a popular place. The rest of the old building was quiet and peaceful as always. Not much had changed since the 1930's when the CCC built this lovely native stone edifice.

Benj ran her hands over the ancient leather bindings stopping randomly and reading the titles. During her time in this little town, Benj had volunteered here, helping Miss

Constance wherever she could. Now the smells and the dust and the wonder of this place came flooding back.

The mystery of Lawnwood and how this very building had helped them solve it. The quirks and twists of Casey's "gifts" came to light right here at this very table. Covered in scars and marks from thousands of kids and students, plodding there way through years of wars and math and English Lit. Benj wondered where the boxes were now. Those infamous boxes that held so many secrets a couple years earlier.

"Well, roll me up and call me a biscuit!" Benj shook herself from her pondering and spun on her heal. Miss Constance stood with the biggest smile she could muster on her old face and her hands on her tiny hips. "Benj!

My girl, my girl!"

Miss Constance closed in and grabbed Benj by the shoulders. The hug was sweet and welcome and smelled of Tabu. "When did you git back in town Honey? My lord it's good to see you!" Miss Constance held on tightly to Benj.

"It's good to see you as well!" Benj said carefully unhooking herself from the tiny woman's grasp.

"Honey you stayin' this time?" The older woman asked hopefully.

"No, I'm afraid I'm just here on vacation. How have you been?" Benj plopped herself in a comfy library chair and patted the one next to her for Miss Constance to sit.

"Oh Honey I'm busier then a cat in a room full of rocking chairs! I got me a high schooler to help out some but you know how that goes." Miss

Constance took off her glasses and started cleaning them.

"They stay till they meet some boy or another, or they just plain disappear! Or they git on them phones they carry and that's the end of the day far as they're concerned. These kids just don't wanna work, especially in some musty ole' library." She tipped her head toward Benj. "I ain't never had the help I had with you Honey, you know that. Things are startin' to get kinda disorderly again and I'm gittin' to old to stop it."

Benj looked sadly at her feet. She could see the dust building up on the shelves just as it was before Benj worked hard to clean it all up. The ancient plaster was back to chipping away on the walls and fluttering down on the books and furniture. As far as Benj was concerned this Library was a town treasure but she wasn't sure anyone else quite saw it that way.

"I love this place." said Benj quietly.

"So do I" said Miss Constance looking around reverently. "Well, one thing we do know is these doors will be open as long as I'm alive to unlock 'em!" Benj chuckled. "Yes it will, I'm sure of that."

Suddenly Miss Constance looked concerned. She placed her wizened old hand on Benj's leg. "Now Benj what's all this I'm hearin' about Casey getting' all wrapped up with another corpse? I swan Honey, I'm not sure all this is quite natural. I'd have to say that young lady needs to steer clear of the dead folks pretty much all together." Miss Constance shook her head and her eyes dropped to her shoes.

"It just ain't right!"

"I know it Miss Constance but this is a little different. Some spook showed up in Casey's bedroom last night and about scared the bejeebers outta both of us." Benj unconsciously ran her fingers through her hair. "This is just all messed up I have to tell you. I'm actually worried about Casey. That's why I wanted to talk to you Ma'am." Benj hung her head.

"Now Honey there has to be a reason that spirit dropped in like that. They don't just pop out of nowhere you know. Gotta be a reason."

Chapter 12

"Come on over here and let me take a better look at that bruise on your arm." Casey gave Miss Ellie the once over and her most threatening look. "How'd you do this anyway?" Casey lightly touched the angry looking bruise on her good friends forearm.

"Oh well Casey I guess I'm jest getting' old is all and I ain't got any excuses for it!" Casey looked at Miss Ellie with a bit of concern. "Does that hurt?" She asked as she pressed a spot on the darkest area.

"Oww! Dang it! O' course it hurts, my arm is injured child don't go pokin' and proddin'. I swear, I question yer sense from time to time."

Casey could barely hold back a

chuckle as she reached for the moisturizing lotion. "If you would use this lotion a little more your skin quality would be better over all ya know." Casey scolded.

"Oh hell I'll let you grease me up when you come round. I like it better when you do it anyway, relaxes me." Casey smiled. "Gonna tell me what happened to cause this?" She said carefully rubbing the softly scented cream over Miss Ellie's skin.

"I decided to make some banana bread for the Chili Supper and Pie Sale overt' the school and I tripped over myself is all."

Casey looked at her with great suspicion. "You tripped over yourself or these damn rugs I've told you to get rid of for the last ten years? Those throw rugs are a fall danger and you and I both know it. Why are you makin' banana bread for a pie sale anyway? Don't they have enough Mama's just a few years younger then you to do that sort of thing?" Casey gave the elderly woman's arm a soft pat and gently released it.

"Thank you Honey that feels so good. My banana bread is famous in this town and you know it. Sold for a good price and made my Grandson very happy. And just maybe not about the Mama's." Miss Ellie flashed Casey a look of concern.

"Seems nobody gives a rats ass about the school doin's anymore, you know that. To much dopin' and drinkin' goin' on around here these days." Miss Ellie dismissed Casey with the sweep of a hand. Casey knew the woman was right about the drugs in this tiny town, it had almost turned into an epidemic.

"Just get rid of the throw rugs will ya or I'm gonna take 'em home myself!" Casey voiced.

"It wasn't that, I just slipped!" Miss Ellie sighed. "Get rid of the rugs or I'll put 'em in my truck right now! Promise me." Casey threatened.

"I like my rugs Casey. I'm not fond of the bare floor." Miss Ellie gave Casey a pitiful look. Casey sighed. "Okay, I'll go get some nonskid backers for them but I do not want to come in here one day and find your brains smashed all over this nice clean kitchen floor cause your a stubborn woman! You hear me?" Casey pointed the finger of guilt at her dear friend.

"Now ain't that just a nice thing to be sayin' to an old woman." Miss Ellie mumbled.

Casey had been doing Home Health for the elderly for over twelve years.

She never once thought this sort of work would be her fate but it suited her well. Casey loved the folks in her care and over time most became as close as family.

"Honey I need you to pluck a couple wiry hairs outta my chin if you got the time."

Casey gave another sideways glance.

"Pull on up here and I'll take a look. Hey, you know anything about that dead kid they found in the old schoolhouse?" Casey asked carefully gripping' the irate whiskers on Miss Ellie chin with a tweezers.

"Oh yeah, I knew that boy. Kinda had a little crush on him, truth be known. But then so did half the school." A wistful smile passed over Miss Ellie's soft face lifting ten years in a second. "He was a cutie patootie!" Miss Ellie rolled an eye Casey's way.

"He had just enough bad in him to stem yer interest." The elderly woman raised an eyebrow at Casey. Casey grinned behind her hand.

"Do you think somebody had it in for him?" Casey asked.

"Dang it girl! Yer tuggin' out half my face!" Miss Ellie hollered and in the same breath started laughing. She slapped her knee and sat back in her chair. "Got ya good din't I? You never hurt me Honey, don't pay me no mind. You have the hands of an angel. Na, I don't think anybody kilt that boy. If yer askin' my opinion I'd say he just got stuck in a bad place in time." Miss Ellie wiped her eyes with a tissue.

"Did I make ya jump?" She asked playfully. The joke was a used one between them but never seemed to get old.

Casey tried her best to look annoyed

but she loved when Miss Ellie teased her.

"Honey, kids used to go up to that third floor and do all sorts of unmentionable things! I'll be honest, I had my first kiss right up there in that very spot. I'd say that boy went up there right as school was closin' up to meet some girl and got stuck up there all summer. That'd be the end a that kid I'd say!"

Casey sat back on her heels. "So that was some sort of make-out spot up there?"

"Well, yeah. Sure was. We called it neckin' back then but I'm sure it's about the same thing. He was all hooked up with Prissy Lou Calvert back then as I recall. Prissy Lou was a mess when he came up missing. Then she came missin' for a bit, completely different reason I'd venture to say."

Casey looked confused. "What does that mean?" She asked.

"I don't wanna go tellin' tales outta school you know, but when girls come into the "family way" back then it was a whole different world then it is now." Casey smiled up at the older woman.

"I think it's a prerequisite for graduating high school now." Casey grinned. Miss Ellie pursed her lips and nodded her head slowly. "Not for none a my Grand-babies it ain't! I'd tan there bottom's sure as livin'!"

Casey carefully slipped Miss Ellie's tweezers back into there holder. "More like Great Grand-babies wouldn't you say?" Casey ran her hand over her friends foot. "Your feet are swollen again. You doin' okay?" She asked lifting her eyes to her friend.

Miss Ellie smiled down at Casey. I'm

fine Honey, just old and gettin' older by the second is all"

Chapter 13

Benj leaned back in the sturdy library chair.

She had spent the afternoon chatting away with her good friend Miss Constance and the hard old wood was making her rear end ache. She felt the chair creak under her weight and let it drop back to the old tile floor.

"I'm not one bit sure whats going on this time to be honest Miss Constance. Casey is scared, I know she is. She's tryin' hard not to let anyone know but she is. I think she kinda believes this "gift" she has is killin' her in some way. The bad part is she's acceptin' it like it's all written in stone or something!" Benj put her elbows on the table and looked across at Miss Constance in a hang-dog way. "It's not like her Ma'am, not one bit." Benj dropped her head and looked pitiful.

"Honey, I think that whole Lawnwood situation took more outta Casey then any of us even knew about. I believe she was honestly hopin' none of this would rear it's ugly head agin." Miss Constance sniffled slightly and pulled an embroidered hanky out of a tiny pocket somewhere in her full skirt.

"What'd that spook want anyway? The one come on in her bedroom?" Miss Constance took off her glasses and wiped her eyes.

Benj shrugged her shoulders. Miss Constance believed herself to be touched with a taste of "The Gift" as well. Hers was nothing like Casey's but sometimes her understanding went much deeper then Benj could ever dream.

"I have no idea Miss C. When she had that little fit in the old school where the ladies first found Ole' Clyde Ray she said she saw a field with a couple little soldier boys in it. Nothing at all to do with poor dead mummified Clyde!"

Miss Constance pounded her small fist on the table. "Let me tell you right here and now those ladies should never have been given that job of goin' thru that rubble in that old schoolhouse! I was against it from the very beginning! I'm on the board you know! Those women are just simply a mess when they get together!" Miss Constance pulled out her hanky and swiped hard at her eye glasses. "You think they're bad now you should have seen them when they were fifteen! Pills! Everyone of them pills and troublemakers. Now don't git me wrong I love each and everyone a them, known 'em my entire life long, Bless there hearts."

The small woman tucked her glasses back on her face and patted her hair.

"There are just some things should be left to others." Miss Constance shuffled and sniffed. "Now about them spooks a Casey's, well Honey, you know that Civil War battle took place out there down 75."

Benj stopped her fidgeting and stared at her friend. "What Civil War battle?" Miss Constance looked a little dumbfounded.

"You mean to say you ain't never heard a the battle out there? My goodness it's almost famous, 'round here anyways. Yep, Battle Of Graves

Creek it was called. Took place out there down about by, well.....your house!"

Benj sat bolt upright. "Our house!" She almost shouted. Miss Constance nodded. "Well, I believe the actual battle took place down a ways, not far though. A bit closer to town on the other side of the highway. Course there was no highway then. Up closer by Clevis Tates place." Miss Constance tapped the table lightly with her fingers. "Tho I'm sure there had to be some action over't your area as well."

Benj sat with her mouth hanging open listening to her friend. "Can you show me? Do you have a book?"

Chapter 14

Casey was halfway down the highway when she remembered the cucumber salad she'd promised Benj. In a few simple moves she'd spun that truck around and was headed back toward the grocery store.

As the electric door wisshed open in front of her, Casey heard a familiar voice shout out her name. "Miss Casey! Miss Casey! Oh my goodness how you been girl?" Casey squinted in the afternoon sun and found herself face to face with one of her former clients. The woman sidled right up and gave her a giant hug.

"How are you Miss Ida May?" Casey asked.

"Oh Honey I ain't doin' any good at

all. What are we standin' out here in the heat for Honey lets go on in the store and cool down!"

The energetic elderly woman swiped her hand in front of the sensor and the door wisshed open once again.

"Now girl I wanted to ask you if you want to sell a couple of those hens a yourn'. I know they lay a fine, fine egg and I'm tired as I can be of these tasteless store bought things! Ya just gotta wonder what they feed those yard birds to get them to lay such generic and sorry cackle-berries." The woman turned toward the dairy section and waved a hand.

"What do you feed your birds to get such tasty treats outta them?" She asked trapping Casey against a tall standing freezer.

"Well, I let them loose so they get

lots of bugs and grubs and I give them table scraps." Casey explained while reaching for the green onions and a couple extra cucumbers.

"Miss Ida May I've got to be on my way I'm afraid. I have a friend in town and I promised her a good meal. I don't really have any chickens for sale. I'm very attached to my birds and want to keep them." Casey started moving slowly toward the registers.

"Casey you gonna tell me you cain't spare a couple of them layers of yours? Good Lord girl it's just you out there on that spread!" Miss Ida May persisted.

"I know Ma'am but I do like eggs, and if you have eggs in your fridge you've got food." Casey slipped the Ida May barrier and started in earnest toward the front of the store.

"Casey! Casey! Just hold up a

second now!" Miss Ida May looked oddly troubled.

"That boy, the boy in the crate?" Casey nodded. "He was my brother."

Chapter 15

Casey almost busked her finger slicing cucumbers. She felt the knife slide down the side just missing her fingernail. "Man, I'd better pay a little more attention before I lose something I may want to use later!" She mumbled to herself. The kitchen smelled of fresh cut veggies and rising yeast bread. "Oh, Benj is gonna eat this meal like it's her very last one!" Casey smiled to herself. Casey loved to cook and was good at it! She cooked for her elderly folks whenever she could and the treats that rolled out of her kitchen were legendary in this tiny town.

At Christmas time Casey collected

coffee cans and covered them in colorful wrapping paper and bows. Then she filled each and every one with cookies and treats to take around town. This week was different tho, she actually got to cook for someone and have then sit down with her to eat. Evening meals were something she missed since Benj had moved away and she was gonna enjoy them while she had her back here again, at least for awhile.

Casey's mind kept wandering back to her strange encounter with Miss Ida May though. The sorrow on that woman's face just broke Casey's heart. She had loved her big brother and the unfinished idea of him just coming up missing was hard to fathom. Casey had known Miss Ida May a long time and had on many occasions considered her a pest.

The old woman was relentless in her desires and demands as were many of Casey's clients but most didn't follow her home and come knockin' on her front door! This new page in Miss Ida's May's story added a different wrinkle to the way Casey pictured it.

Funny thing is the woman just didn't know how to simply ask the questions she wanted answers to. She had to hem and haw and tip toe around everything like so many folks of that generation. Casey loved the WWII generation and appreciated the job they had done for this country, but some of those old ways she was glad to see disappear with nightly curlers and seamed nylon hose.

A big smile broke across Casey's face and her heart skipped a beat as she heard the front door rattle and slam open.

"Nothin' like a subtle entrance for you huh Benj?" Casey teased. "I can't even believe you drove the golf cart into town today! I sorta can't believe it made it that far!" Benj sauntered into the fragrant kitchen and grabbed a slice of cucumber out of Casey's bowl.

"Oh that cart would prolly make it to Ada if it was charged enough! I had fun on the old thing." Benj reached out for another slice of cuke but got her hand slapped in the process.

"Stop it! Those are salted! They've gotta be kinda nasty! Just wait till I get the salad made will ya! If your hungry there's some sliced strawberries in the fridge, eat those." Benj pulled out a chair and plopped down.

"Man, it smells so good in here girl! What's for supper anyway?"

The girls had used the 1970's era

golf cart around the farm relentlessly. It had hauled hay and feed on it's duck taped seats and rolled over acres of land on it's unmatched tires. Since Benj had been gone the old cart had sat silently in the shed unused and unloved. Casey knew Benj would have the thing out and charged before her vacation was over, she just didn't know it would be this soon!

"Did you plug the cart back in?" Casey asked "Of course I did! It my number one mode of transport while I'm here. Gotta keep it movin' don't I? What's for dinner?" Benj asked wandering to the fridge and taking out the bowl of strawberries. She rolled a hefty berry in the sugar bowl and popped it in her mouth.

"Boy, Casey, do we have a lot to talk about!" Casey glanced up at her friend.

"What do you mean?" she asked.

"I spent some time at the library today with Miss Constance...." Casey reached into the cupboard and pulled down a small bowl. She spooned out some sugar and placed it in front of Benj taking the sugar bowl away from her completely and flashing a filthy look Benj's way.

"What does that mean? I haven't been to the library since the whole Lawnwood thing happened. How is Miss Constance anyway? I have to admit I'm a little hesitant to go back there." Casey shook a few stray strawberry seeds out of the sugar bowl and put the lid back on. "I guess I shouldn't feel that way. Miss Constance was just wonderful to me and I don't want to be an ass." Casey mused.

"Oh she's just dandy." replied Benj.

"She gave me a lot of info we might find quite interesting. Your not an ass Case. Miss Constance understands a lot more then you think. Remember she fancies herself to have the same 'gift' you have." Benj reached into the pocket of her jeans and pulled out a pile of neatly folded papers. "We can go over this stuff after we eat, now...what's for supper I'm about to starve where I stand and I'm getting' no answers outta you!"

Chapter 16

"Whoa!" Casey exclaimed. "I had no idea all this was going on right here by our house." She pushed one of the papers Benj copied from the Library to the side.

"We have to go over there Benj." Casey shoved her glasses further up on her nose. " I swear! I think this is the key to everything! Why didn't we know about this? I've been living here for thirteen years for Gods sake! Who knew there was a battlefield right across the roadway."

Benj glanced at her friend. "I'm not sure going over there is the answer Case. I mean, who knows what kind of effect that'll have on you...I can only imagine." Benj turned slightly pale in the fading sunlight.

"Besides Mr. Tate is no walk in the park, he's a mean old man and no one to tangle with."

Benj brushed a sprinkling of crumbs off the arm of the sofa she was sitting on. "Man, those cookies are good! Do we have any left? How did you have time to make this wonderful meal and cookies as well? You really have denied your true callin' Casey." Casey gave Benj a stern look over the top of her glasses.

"Should I be barefoot and pregnant as well?" She mumbled.

"Stop it Case! You know what I mean! Your a fantastic cook and you plan things just so, it's an amazing thing....where are those cookies?" Benj scooted off the sofa and wandered toward the kitchen.

"How 'bout we just start by drivin'

past that area over there? We could do that without me fallin' into some sort of fit don't you think? Stop rummaging' around in there! The cookies are in the cookie jar!" Casey shouted.

"The canister?' Benj asked. "People don't really use canisters Casey. They are strictly for show." Casey smiled to herself as she heard the distinct sound of the cookie jar lid being lifted.

"Miss Nell made those canisters for me over at the Indian Center, and I'm gonna use 'em." Casey stretched out her legs and stared up at the ceiling.

This was her favorite time of the day. Chores were done, dishes put up and the house was tidy. The Oklahoma sun was struggling hard to win it's battle with the soft impending darkness and it filled Casey's ancient living room with deep and brilliant shadows.

"We could go now." Casey said sighing deeply. "What?" Benj replied crumbs bouncing off her lower lip.

"It's almost dark Casey. We are not gonna go traipsing over there in the dark, that man would shoot us dead!" Benj flashed a irritated look in Casey's direction.

"Benj, it's not like we're drivin' twenty miles down the highway for Godsake. It's across the street!" Benj plopped herself back into the sofa making it clear that was exactly where she was going to stay.

"No." She mumbled letting another crumb drop from her lip.

…..........

Casey waved at Mrs Shuckey as she drove her truck slowly down Main Street. The elderly woman returned the wave and a big smile flashed across her worn old face. Casey loved this tiny town. Oh, she realized things were changing and for as long as she had lived here the town had dried up a little more every year. At one time this little prairie haven sported three movie houses and four grocery stores. Now there was one lone store and the bright marquees and smell of fresh popcorn were somewhere deep in the memories of the people still hanging on.

Casey wound the big truck into the parking lot of the store and sat quietly smiling to herself as she watched her world pass in front of her. She firmly believed if you hung around this store long enough you would see everyone you knew and hear all the latest goin's on worth hearing. As Casey finally threw a leg out the door of her pick-up she spotted Miss Evelyn struggling with her cane and a hefty Black Beauty watermelon, the watermelon was winning.

"Hey Miss Evelyn how's this fine day treatin' you?" Casey asked grabbing the melon out of the woman's hands and setting in the front seat of her Oldsmobile.

"Why thank you Casey. I was just about the lose the fight with that bugger!" Miss Evelyn patted Casey on the shoulder and swung her giant purse in next to the misbehaving melon in the front seat.

"Is Mr Essa gonna be home to heft that for you?" Casey asked, slowly helping the women to the drivers door.

"Oh he's home alright. He's always home. Essa's been retired from the Railroad for the last twenty years and he's been underfoot every minute a that." The woman patted Casey again.

"You need me to follow you home and help you with the groceries?" Casey asked.

"No Sweetie, Mary Elizabeth's comin' by in awhile. I'll wait on her to carry that monster in fer me." Casey grinned.

"That'll work Miss Evelyn, but gotta get that thing in the fridge! Just no good if it ain't cold! You be careful drivin' home now." Casey turned to go into the sliding doors of the store.

"Casey we ain't been back up to the school since...well, you know...the incident. Don't think I'm goin' back a'tall. Don't think my old heart could take that." Casey leaned against the aging Oldsmobile.

"No, you ladies have done enough up there I'd say." Miss Evelyn started her car with a low deep rumble. "Tell Mary Elizabeth hello!" Casey shouted as the big car slowly eased out of the parking space. Miss Evelyn waved and slowly rolled the big boat of a car into only four way stop in town.

Chapter 17

   Casey rolled down Main Street sipping on an icy Dr Pepper. Her last client had a doctors appointment so she was free for a couple hours. This was one of the drawbacks of living out of town, going home in the middle of the day was inconvenient but Casey wouldn't have it any other way. She happily rolled through the quiet streets of her town listening to music and tapping the beat on her steering wheel.

   She thought about visiting her buddy Miss Ellie but decided she didn't want to be pesky.

   Before Casey was aware of which way her truck was traveling, the stately old High School building loomed large in her windshield.

Casey remembered what Miss Evelyn had said moments ago. Casey pulled her pick-up into the circle drive that lead to the tall brass portico. She turned the radio down and stared at the old building.

"Oh what the hell, I've got a couple of hours!" She said to herself pushing the door open and swinging out to the scared and age-dimpled concrete drive.

"What do you have to tell me you big dead hulk of a building?" Casey mumbled as she craned her neck and stared up. The empty windows looked black and imposing as she slowly scanned the stone facade.

"Oh the years of kids that did this very thing everyday." she thought.

"Yelling and laughing and dreading they're lack of finished

homework. Friends piling in cars at this very curb looking forward to an afternoon at the pool hall and burger joint in town. Girls in bobby socks and flared out skirts with letter jackets slipped casually over there shoulders. Letter jackets with leather sleeves and the school colors. Letter jackets just like the one that kid was wearing, that kid in the crate.

Casey tugged on the heavy brass door and to her surprise it swung open.

"Why isn't this locked?" she asked herself.

"I'm gonna have to call someone about this." She mumbled as she stepped into the cool, darkness of the main floor hallway. Casey let her eyes adjust to the semi-darkness for just a minute. She sniffed the air around her. Shinning dust glitter twinkled in the rays of sunlight. Ancient chalk powdered it's way into her nostrils.

"Man, this school is so much like the one I went to." Casey mumbled.

As she stepped into the vestibule the staircases started. One on either side, "Boy's staircase and Girls staircase on the other side. Both were winding and grand in there own way.

Casey glanced down the long hallways the darkness broken only by the sunlight filtering dimly through dusty classroom windows. Casey smiled to herself as she heard the sounds of thousands of teenagers laughing and bustling to a thousand different destinations. The sounds tumbled and rolled like a slow freighter easing into Casey's consciousness like a wayward drip. She watched as the tiny partials of dust formed into squirming, happy students from year after year of surviving high school trauma.

The halls were packed with kids dressed in skirts and blouses from the thirty's and forty's to the form hugging jeans of the sixty's.

Casey watched in fascination at the swarm of crew cut, long haired pegged jeaned, bell bottomed mass passing in shadows before her.

Suddenly Casey realized these happy carefree kids had all passed from this life in one way or the next. There were wars to be fought and car wrecks. Some fell to illness and some took there own flame. Some simply grew old and worn and left with satisfaction. She felt honored to have this single moment of retreating childhood with them once again.

Casey's eyes filled as she lowered her head and ran her hand along the highly varnished wooden rail. Casey turned and made her way up the long staircase, making sure she chose the "Girls" side.

The sounds quickly faded as she climbed the well worn risers. Each step creaked a little under her sneakers. Casey remembered her days in high school, learning which stairs creaked so the hall monitors wouldn't hear her. Casey unconsciously started walking the pattern she knew so well. The second floor landing brought her to a stop as somewhere in time a bell rang and once again kids tumbled out the classrooms banging the doors loudly on there speedy way to somewhere.

Lockers slammed and boys leaned on whatever they could to chat up girls. Casey saw a young girl with big, soft blue eyes, reaching into a locker with a skinny boy helping out all he could. His hair was dark and slicked back and he balanced a pair of wire framed glasses on his crooked nose. The girl was small and pretty with an easy smile. Casey leaned hard against the wall behind her. "Mr Dunbar." Casey whispered in awe.

Casey had loved a client of hers deeply. A man well into his ninety's. She loved him like he was family. She cared for him until he had passed just months before. Now here he was...young and skinny and making a show for some girl. Casey watched as he took the girls books and they walked arm and arm directly past her. They didn't know just then that war would come and babies and through it all they would continue to walk arm in arm. Casey reached out her hand but she couldn't touch them.

Gone was the smell of old man, sickness and impending death. Casey almost laughed out loud as she breathed in the clean smell of healthy boy, jam packed with hormones and vinegar. "You go Mr Dunbar!" Casey whispered as she watched them fade into a mist down the hallway.

The third floor was different somehow, she felt it right away. It almost didn't seem like a part of this school. Things seemed much older and more worn up here. The musty smell was strong and the hallways were empty. Casey glanced into the tiny girls bathroom. The sink was chipped and broken and the door to the single stall was hanging on one hinge. Every surface was covered in paint chips and a heavy layer of dust. Casey's heart beat faster as she hesitantly dragged herself toward the end of the hallway.

It was very dark up here at the top of this old building. Casey wanted to turn and scurry down the stairs and out into the afternoon sunlight. She told herself there was nothing to touch, nothing to send her into another excursion into the unknown. It was all taken away now. It was over. She steadied herself against a bank of steel lockers. A female voice giggled in front of her. The dark hall seemed to suddenly go even darker. Casey's eyes took a moment to adjust. Leaning against an ancient crate she saw two figures in the dim light. They were talking softly and it became apparent some sort of wooing was going on. Casey strained to hear. The boy reached over and brushed his hand through the young girls wavy auburn hair. Her nervous laughter lilted softly. She pushed her hair back with her hand and gently pushed the boys fingers away. The boy turned slightly and Casey recognized him as the kid in the crate, that crate! The crate they were leaning against. The boy dropped his hand to the girls thigh.

Once again she pushed him away. He laughed. "You cain't push me away girly!" The boy laughed again. "You ain't nothin' but trash. You should be happy I'm even up here with the likes a you!" Casey watched horrified...she knew her. She knew that face, yes...it was older, much older... but it was the very same face.

Chapter 18

"Do you want me to fry up some okra for supper tonight?" Casey asked Benj as she sat in her cozy kitchen.

"Is the Pope Catholic? Do snakes come out in tall grass? Of course I want okra while I'm in Oklahoma! It's not dinner without fried okra, chicken fried steak and corn bread now is it?" Benj asked as she swung herself into the vinyl kitchen chair.

Benj noticed right away Casey's eyes were rimmed in dark circles and her hands were shaking slightly.

"They had some beautiful okra over at the market today, couldn't pass it up." Casey said trying hard to look unaffected. "Dinner will be ready in a few minutes why don't you go on out and play with the sheep before the bugs get bad? It's a lovely evening and the dogs could stand to have you rough 'em up a bit." Casey looked at Benj guiltily.

"Oh yeah, that sounds like a great idea, and when I get back in here and we sit down for dinner you can tell me all about what you've been up to today. Can't you Casey?" Casey rolled her eyes. Sometimes Benj just knew her way to well.

"You look like you've seen a ghost. A statement that somehow loses much of its affect on you." Benj said giving Casey the sideways look. "I'm gonna go play now but you got some 'spalinin' to do Lucy!"

After the dishes were done and they were parked in the cozy old living room. Casey put her head back against the worn sofa.

"You want a cup a coffee or a soda?" she asked.

"Spill it." replied Benj. Casey lowered her chin to her chest and a short sob escaped from her.

"Damn it Benj I'm tired. I'm just so tired of all this shit. I want things to go back to what they were before Lawnwood...back to normal."

A lone tear skidded down Casey's cheek as she raised her tired eyes to her friend.

"I'm scared to go in my own bedroom in case the damn Southern Militia is camping out in some corner..not to mention dead kids in old crates! Jesus Christ! Enough...Not only that but your leaving soon! Again!"

Casey slapped her hand on her forehead and raggedly sobbed.

Benj just couldn't take it when

Casey cried. She had no idea what to do. Her heart was torn from here to there when Casey was hurting. Casey was a strong woman and things rarely piled up on her like this.

"We'll work it out Casey. Casey? You listening to me? We'll get it all squared away. Tell you what, I'll stay another week how's that? I've got the time comin' and I think you need me here more then my bathroom needs painting. How's that? Does that work?"

Casey turned her tear stained face toward Benj and tried hard to smile. "I went to the high school today." she whispered.

"I want so badly to be pissed at you!" steamed Benj. "But I can't be pissed when your in such sorrow." Casey had explained her day to Benj as best she could, leaving out the girls identity in her narrative. The tears were coming like an afternoon rain and as Casey spoke her body shuddered slightly.

Benj was more then worried. Casey sniffled and wiped her sunken eyes. Benj wandered to the kitchen and got a roll of paper towels.

"Here, blow your nose." She said roughly. "You can come in and sleep with me tonight, the sixth army won't go in my room...I hope. Come on, go wash your face and get your PJ's on, it'll be fine." Benj reassured her friend but in her heart she just wasn't sure.

Morning came without incident.

Heat rippled across the asphalt in waves and mirages of puddles. The sky was a crystal azure blue.

"Weather comin'!" The old man stirred his coffee and wrapped his fingers around the heavy ceramic cup.

"Yep." mumbled another.

Every morning for the past hundred years a gaggle of elderly gentlemen had nursed cups of coffee together in this very spot. Their hands were scared and faces work weary. They all had some sort of hat pulled low over there sun burnt brows. Old caps advertising seed or broken felt hats fit precisely by age and wear. They had put in there time in the oil fields and on family farms, or both. Now they met before dawn broke every morning to nurse coffee and shoot the shit, exactly as there fathers and grandfathers had done before them.

"Were needin' the rain." someone mumbled.

"Yep, maybe more'n just rain tho. Gotta watch'n see." They all turned there heads slightly and squinted out the big front window of the diner currently wrapped around them.

"Yep, could be sumphin'. Darleen, Honey can I git a warm up over here?"

Casey slid the worn wooden door open and slipped in to the slightly dim diner.

"Hey Miss Casey!" A friendly voice boomed from behind the open counter that was covered to brimmin' with plates of greasy eggs and bacon.

"Hey, Leon!" Casey hollered back.

"Girl, git yerself a cup a that coffee and sit a minute fore' you go runnin' off to git after yer day!" The handsome older man tipped the paper cap back on his balding head and gave Casey a gold toothed grin. She slid herself on to a cracked stool that bellied up to the lunch counter. Casey loved this old place. She knew it had been open just about as long as this state itself and that pleased her.

Now and again she had to blink away the shadowy occupants that somehow always insisted on staying. Casey didn't mind. They were roughnecks and cowboys that loved this greasy little diner for all the years of it's life. They belonged here just as much as Casey herself did.

Casey walked to the giant coffeemaker and filled two foam cups to the brim.

"Hey Leon!" She shouted. "I'm getting' two cups to go for me and Chester, okay?"

"Chester! That dirty ole' scoundrel!

How's he holdin' up anyway?" Casey watched as the mans friendly face peeked around the corner at her.

"He's okay, needs to exercise more so he can walk better, but he's good." Casey stirred several spoons of sugar into the cups and snapped on the plastic lids.

"Honey, we all need to exercise a little more! Tell that old man to mind you or I'm a gonna come on over there and give him what for!" Leon Chifford expertly flipped a pancake and two eggs in the blink of an eye.

"You want me to make him up some eggs real quick?' The man asked. "I know he ain't eatin' right. I seen him in the Dollar General the other day and he looked frail." Leon leaned on the counter and asked earnestly.

"Na, not today Leon but thank you. Chester hasn't been eatin' good. I'll just make him some oatmeal when I get over there." Casey lifted the foam cups toward the man behind the counter. "Put these on my tab will ya?" Casey asked. Leon burst into friendly laughter...

"Kid don't you insult me! Git on outta here! Tell Chester I'm coming to whip his ass at some domino's later in the week!" Casey laughed. Leon hadn't taken money from her for years now, at least when it came to his old friend Chester.

"I'll deliver the message Leon! Thanks." Casey pushed out the door and almost bumped a cowboy dressed in full range gear....but he melted away as Casey held the door for him.

The day was still as the tomb and the hot cups of coffee were making rivlets of sweat run down Casey's face. She glanced up at the white hot sky.

"Weather Comin'!" She whispered to herself.

"I brought you coffee from Leon." Casey announced as she helped Chester sit up in bed.

"That ole' coot say anything?" Chester asked giving Casey a corner of the eye look.

"O' course he did! You know damn well I can't get out the door of that place without getting' some sort of flack offa that guy." Casey carefully steadied the old gentleman as he coaxed himself into his power chair.

"The guy ain't nothin' but a bag a wind and he knows it well as I do." Chester hoisted the cup to his lips and took a long sip of the steaming liquid.

"Makes a hell of a cup a coffee tho, I'll give him that." Chester leaned back in his chair and closed his eyes. "We were a damn good basketball team back in the day tho girl. That goes without sayin'." Chester winked a dark brown eye at Casey.

"Your getting a bath today Mister so brace yourself. I swear Chester I'm gonna burn that t-shirt your wearing! I could make soup out of it with everything you've spilled. Leon says he's gonna whip your ass at dominoes later in the week by the way. " Casey added.

"Ha! That'll be the day!" Chester replied laughing.

"Hey Chester?" Casey asked grabbing a clean towel from the bathroom. "Did you play basketball with Clyde Ray Trummel?" Casey laid the clean towel over the back of Chester's chair.

"Asshole." Chester mumbled softly.

"What? Tell me what you really

think Chester!" Exclaimed Casey.

"That kid was an asshole." Chester sipped his coffee slowly. "Thought his shit didn't stink. Thought he was the slickest guy in town. His Daddy was the Postmaster you know." Chester raised one eyebrow toward Casey.

"Government job. They had a little jingle I guess..a little morn' most. But the guy was a jerk. Could sink a basketball but that was about all he could do." Chester cleared his throat. "I wasn't sorry when he come up missin'." Chester looked up at Casey. "Prolly go to hell for that statement. We gonna do this bath or you just gonna sit there and wool gather?" Casey tapped the old man playfully on the shoulder.

"I'm sure there's much more your goin' to Hell for then that! Lets get to it Buddy!" Casey smiled.

Chapter 19

Benj sat sprattle legged on the front porch. Her feet dangling down the short flight of stairs. The day was quiet but nowhere near peaceful.

"Weather comin'." She mumbled to herself. She took out a cigarette and lit it. She watched the paper burn away around the tobacco. Benj's mind was everywhere but here on this porch. She watched the chickens run around to the front of the house and stand in front of her cocking there heads and watching her from one eye then the next.
Benj smiled a sad little smile at the friendly birds. Her and Casey had driven all the way to Tulsa and bought

these hens all the way back when she was living here on a more permanent basis. She remembered how angry she had gotten when Casey had taken a wrong turn and they had gotten lost coming home. It was well after dark when they settled the tiny birds in there new home. Casey had gone to bed without speaking to her. Benj sat on the back porch with her 410 between her knees watching for predators.

She was hard on Casey back then, she knew she was being a jerk and didn't want to be. Casey was kind to a fault and now she was out here in the wild alone. Benj tried hard not to think about it to often.

One of the fat little Rhode Island Reds jumped up into Benj's lap and settled down to be petted.

"Damnit Karen! Casey's got you so

spoiled you'd walk right up to a coyote!" Benj ran her hand over the soft red feathers and the little hen cooed. Benj couldn't help but grin. She took that last puff off her forgotten cigarette and stubbed it out on the porch rail making sure no ember survived.

'That's all I need to do isn't it girl." Benj asked the sleepy little hen. "Burn her damn house down!" She watched the sun rolling a brilliant orange as it dropped into the trees out past Yeager.

"Come on girls!" Benj said tucking Karen under her arm. "I'll walk you back to the hen house before Casey putters in and stirs the pot. "I may take that woman out for Chinese tonight. Think she'd like that?" Benj asked the chickens. "Oh, I think she would. Come on now."

"Oh my God Benj that was so friggin' good!" Casey pushed her self away from the table taking one last nibble at her Spicy Orange Beef. "What got into you? Oh shit, I don't even care! I like it!" Casey was all smiles as the waitress brought a little tray of fortune cookies.

"I just thought I'd take you out for once is all." Benj loved seeing Casey so happy. This life had grated on her in the last few years and there was little relief.

"You wanna go throw a couple bucks around over't the casino for a bit before we go home?" Benj asked feeling full and good.

"Na, why don't we just get in the truck and drive around the back roads for awhile, see what we can find. You can drive, I'm kinda sick of it." Casey cracked open her fortune cookie and read aloud.

"Your fortune is your pleasure." Hmmm....what fortune would that be?" She grinned across the table at her friend. "Read yours!" Benj cracked hers open and popped half a cookie in her mouth.

"Consider your time and use it well." Both women looked at each other playfully.

"In bed!" They said in unison, laughing. A low rumble made them both turn there faces to the window.

"Maybe we should think about drivin' around another evening." Casey said thoughtfully. "Weather comin'.....fast!"
Benj shook her head in agreement.

"Maybe we'd better just head for the house, ya think?" Casey shook her head in agreement.

"Probably." She took the last sip of her Diet Dr Pepper.

"Benj, do you think the weather has anything to do with this...thing, whatever it is that I can do?" Casey looked earnestly across the table at her friend.

"I don't know, why do you say that?" answered Benj pulling on her hoodie.

"Man, I've been seein' dead folks all over the place today."

The sky was dark and foreboding as they pulled into the drive. The rain was starting to pelt the truck with a vengeance. A chill was starting to sink deep into the woman's bones as they watched the barnyard light start to wink on and off.

"Well, we'd better take a run for it while we can! Looks like we're gonna lose power any second!" A loud crash of thunder crashed and the sky broke into a million pieces as lightening shattered the static blackness. The strong smell of ozone wafted through the air promising more...more storm, more violence from above. The sky broke again and a million cracks appeared above them brilliantly breaking the heavens like onyx crystal. Benj slammed open the truck door and shouted.

"Run Casey, Run!"

They met again at the front door soaked through to the skin and laughing. Suddenly a lightening strike snapped at the transformer out at the highway. The explosion was deafening and sparks flew over the spruce and ceder trees lining the drive.

"Holy Shit!" shouted Casey as the transformer caught fire for the a second or two. The barn yard light cracked as well and died leaving them in pitch darkness.

"You got your keys? Open the door Case!" Benj shouted over the frey. Casey fumbled with the door and they tumbled into the comfort of home...

Chapter 20

"Casey grab a flashlight!" Benj whispered. "Can't see a friggin' thing in this house!" Casey ran her hands over the kitchen counter till she reached the little penlight she kept there. When she snapped it on a soft yellow light weakly shone.

"What the hell is that?" Benj laughed. "Geeze, a match would throw more light then that thing!" Casey smiled knowing that statement was absolutely true.

"Just hold up." She laughed. "I've got some oil lamps in the cupboard." Soon the room was filled with a lovely glow from the tall chimney's smoking lightly on the table.

"Good Lord don't let the cats get at

those things!" Benj exclaimed. "Why exactly don't you have a decent flashlight? Why do you insist on living like it's 1864? There are LED lights now Casey and they would fill this room just like electric, but..here we are." Benj dropped heavily on the comfy old sofa.

"I like the lamps." stated Casey. "They have a lovely feel to them don't they?" Benj looked around the room at the deep shadows cast by the flickering oil lamps.

"It's creepy." She announced. "And it's dangerous around the animals." Benj tucked a pillow under her head and swung her feet up. "Wanna tell ghost stories?" She teased.

"Shut up!" muttered Casey trying hard not to smile. The storm raged and hollered outside the old house like a demon loosed. "I'm gonna go take a fast shower before the water goes cold." stated Casey picking up one of the lamps. "Hold down the fort while I'm in there will ya?" Benj closed her eyes and smiled.

"You shouldn't take a shower during a storm." She said sleepily.

"I'll be out in five minutes." said Casey as she rounded the corner into the hallway.

Casey stood in the cooling water in pitch darkness broken only by the flickering light of her oil lamp. She let the water soothe some of the cares out of her heart. It was a strange sensation scrubbing down in the darkness, but Casey liked it. She could hear the storm outside the window and the house shook slightly from time to time as the wind gusted.   After slipping into some clean PJ's she wandered down the dark hallway holding her lamp in front of her. As she traveled through the old kitchen she noticed the cabinet was open just a crack and out peered several sets of glowing eyes.

"Cowards!" Casey mumbled toward her cowering cats. She joined Benj back in the living room running her fingers through her wet hair. Benj was curled into a ball with several more scarred cats tucked around her, sound asleep. Casey fluffed Benj's short dark hair and pulled a crocheted afghan over her. As she turned to go to her room she cupped her hand over the top of the lamp and blew hard. The lamp smoked lightly and extinguished. She left her bedroom door open a few inches in case Benj woke and didn't realize the lights were out. Then she turned back the covers and climbed into her bed.

"Madam!" Casey started just a little as she woke in the thick darkness. "Madam!" Casey heard again. All around her the air felt charged and heavy. Casey remembered the storm that was raging as she slept and thought this was just a side effect of that event. She rested her head back on her familiar pillow and once again shut her eyes.

"Madam you must wake!" This time Casey's eye's popped open. She sat up on one elbow feeling confused and lightheaded.

"Who are you?" Casey whispered. Suddenly a lightening flash lit the room in a wash of pale blue light. In the corner stood a stooped figure in a battered uniform. Casey thought about Benj sound asleep just on the other side of the partially open door.

"Madam, I will not harm you. I am here for your assistance." The figure didn't move or seem to speak but Casey could hear him clearly. He spoke with a slow, careful. educated Southern drawl.

"Madam I wish you to accompany me tonight. If you do you will find the answers you seek." The figure stood stock still disappearing and appearing as the lightening flashed.

"What do you mean follow you? I'm not going anywhere in this storm!" Casey sat bolt upright.

"Hey Case! You okay in there?" Benj hollered from the living room. Just then the lights popped on and the whole house was filled with warm, welcome light.

Benj appeared in Casey's doorway dragging the afghan behind her. "Who are you talkin' to?" Benj's hair was standing up all over her head and her face carried the pattern of the afghan she was curled up in.

"You got another spook in there?" Benj asked. Casey smiled at her disheveled friend.

"Well, yeah...as a matter of fact I did!"

The following morning as the girls sleepily sipped good, hot coffee, the sun was shining like a beacon thru the old double pained windows.

"Man that yards a mess with that gully washer last night. The sheep are ankle deep in mud and you don't even wanna see those 'supposed' to be white, dogs." Benj mumbled half to herself.

Casey halfheartedly smiled and ran her fingers thru her hair. Benj turned and looked at her friend. Casey looked beat all to hell on this bright, sunny day. Her face was drawn and her hands shook slightly around the big ole' mug she cradled.

"Okay, here's the deal." Benj popped a slice of toast into her mouth and chewed loudly. Tomorrow is Saturday. We'll get up in the bright light of day and drive on over there to the so called 'battlefield'. I'll be right with you in case you need saving...which knowing you will probably be the situation. It'll be the brightest part of the day. None of this dead of night or ragin' storm business." Benj grabbed a slice of peach and popped it in her mouth along with the toast.

"Oh man! Good peaches! Where did you get those?" She exclaimed. "That way we'll both be safe and we can finally find out what exactly this damn spook wants! Deal?" Benj glanced at Casey grinning. Casey's eyes were rimmed in bluish circles. Her hand trembled slightly as she brought her cup to her lips and nodded agreeing with Benj's plan. "Deal" she said weakly.

Chapter 21

Saturday came knockin' with a burst of sunshine and the clean smell only a good stiff rainstorm can muster. Casey woke to shy sunshine inchin' it's way into her bedroom window. She stretched and yawned and rolled over careful not to disturb her little cat and partner in sleeping. In the back of Casey's mind a deep sadness started to build. She closed her eyes quickly and squinched them tight, but it was no use at all. A little tear oozed out and found her warm morning cheek to roll down. Casey laid quietly holding her purring kitty tight to her. Benj would be leaving soon.

Casey knew the next few days would be eventful. But in her mind the biggest event of all would be smiling and waving, then turning to walk, once again, into an empty house.

She heard rustling from the back bedroom and the toilet flush. She heard Benj chatting with the cats as she shuffled through the old house trying to be quiet. Quiet was not something Benj had a real strong grasp of, especially if there was adventure on the horizon.

Casey could smell coffee brewing and she winced to herself. Benj's coffee could melt a spoon. Once again Casey stretched and sat her rumbling friend aside as she swung her legs over the side of the bed and loosed herself from the quilt Miss Offy had made her.

"Benj?" She shouted. "That better not be coffee I smell! Damn, that stuff will be eatin' through the counter before I haul my carcass in their!" She listened to Benj mumbling and cursing as she headed out the bedroom door, the promise of a good day just a fingers length away.

"We could take the golf cart." mentioned Benj as she munched the end off a piece of wonderful bacon.

"You know what Case?" Casey raised an eyebrow toward her friend. "You just can't get bacon like this in Chicago. It simply is not possible." Benj shook her head and took another small nibble.

"It's Blue And Gold that's why." explained Casey as she sat a plate of steaming pancakes in front of her friend. "It comes from the FFA kids. They only sell it once a year so you have to snap it right up!" Casey slide down in the facing chair and grabbed several crispy pieces of bacon for herself. "You'd sit there and eat every slice wouldn't you?" She asked waving a chunk of bacon in front of Benj's face.

"I might, I am the guest you know!" said Benj grabbing the treat from Casey's hand and popping it in her mouth.

"Oh guest my oversized ass! Your just a pig plain and simple!" Benj grinned and both women burst into laughter.

"So, what's the plan Stan?" Casey said giving Benj a good natured shove in the head.

"I'm not exactly sure, but...I think we should just wander over there, casually. Give the place a once over. If all goes well we can take it from there. What do you think?"

Casey brushed some wayward

crumbs off the tablecloth.

"Well, I don't think we should take the golf cart. I would like something solid around me just in case. That slow movin' little hoopdy just ain't gonna cut it today!"

"Okay, okay..I'll agree with that. Little stability in the transport is a good thing, we'll take your truck then." Benj popped a chunk of dripping pancakes in her mouth and closed her eyes in absolute rapture.

"Damn Casey!" Benj leaned back in her chair and let the sweet goodness melt into her. I swear girl you missed your calling completely! Before I came here I'd never had pancakes from scratch, now you've ruined me forever. All other pancakes pale in comparison."

Casey watched this drama from across the table. "I cook everyday silly chick!"

Benj opened her eyes. "For old people! You cook for a bunch of elderly folk! You should be cookin' for Royalty! You should have a fancy restaurant somewhere in the city, I swear!"

Casey grinned from ear to ear, just a touch of stress draining away. Benj could always warm her heart. "I'm not sure my pancakes could rate the Royal treatment." Casey laughed.

"Don't underestimate the power of a fluffy pancake my sister!" mused Benj.

"Grab a couple bottles of water will ya?" screamed Casey. "I've got the Styrofoam cooler in here so it'll stay cold."

Benj wandered to the porch and

glared at her friend. "Casey, we are driving across the highway! You can see where we're going from here for God sake! This is not a Safari! This is not a cross country road trip! If we need a drink of water we can just come the hell home and get one! Geezer Case, sit down and chill a minute. I'll drive the damn truck! Your shakin' like you've seen a ghost." Benj smirked and quickly turned her head to keep from laughing. Casey plopped on the front step and sighed heavily.

"I'm a wreck." she explained. "Sorry. I sorta feel like I'm being lowered in a tank of sharks without a cage around me."

Benj dropped down next to Casey on the step. "We aren't gonna do anything today but look Case. That's all. I promise."

Chapter 22

The day was a beautiful scorcher. You could almost watch the grass as it stretched it's little green legs and reached for the sun. You could wade through the thick air sucking in gallons of water along your way. Sweat beaded off Casey and Benj's foreheads before they even started there adventure.

"Dang it's hot!" mumbled Benj wiping away a stray trickle. "You know you almost forget what Oklahoma summers are like when you leave. I guess it's like that with everything though. You just kinda pick and choose the very best stuff and let the rest float away out of your mind." Benj took a sneaky look over at Casey. She was staring out the truck window, her face blank and drawn. Benj was a little shocked at how much Casey had aged in the last year. All this spook stuff had certainly taken it's toll on her friend.

"We gonna sit and wool gather or are you gonna start this truck?" Casey asked looking in wonder at her friend. "Where did you wander off to just then Benj? You were as spaced as a badly written sentence." Casey patted her friend on the knee and motioned for her to turn the key. "Won't start unless you do that." She said smiling. The old truck roared to life without hesitation. Casey held her breath the whole three and a half minutes it took to get to their destination. The beautiful field of blue-stem swayed in the warm Oklahoma breeze as the truck creeped over yet another rise. Casey watched out the passenger window finally gasping and sucking in the hot, moist air. "Go slow, Benj..." Casey instructed. "If I go any slower we're gonna be walkin' it." Benj mumbled.

    Casey squinted her eyes and focused on the tiny stream bubbling down the lush pasture. She saw a tree filled to brimming with horse apples and a few peaceful cattle enjoying the morning sunshine. Suddenly the truck disappeared around her and the gravel road was gone. The wind wafted toward her with a smell she barely knew or recognized. She lifted her chin and cocked her head and a look of confusion crossed her face. The smell hit her once again. Wood fire and gunpowder. Fear struck Casey like a bat across her shoulders. She strained her eyes to see up on the ridge where two half grown boys stepped for all eternity into her vision. Tears and smoke burned her cheeks as she tried to motion, tried to cry out. She watched as the boys wrestled and goofed like puppies in the tall grass.

"Casey!" Somewhere in the back of her brain she heard her friends voice. "Casey! For the love a God wake up! Damn it Casey! Snap the hell outta it! Please!" Casey felt a stream of something liquid and warm trickle down her face. The sky was as blue cornflowers as it spun above her.

"Casey! Come on...please, please wake up!"

The voice was louder now and more insistent.

"Benj?" Casey asked in a small voice. "Why are you here?" Casey put her hand to her head and felt wetness there.

"Come on Case, we have to get you to the hospital! You have to stand up I can't lift you in the truck!" Casey slowly stood, her head spinning.

"Benj, why are you here?"

"Why am I where? We came out here so you could check things out remember?" We drove over here from the house. Look Case!" Benj pointed across the highway where you could barely see the old house. Casey stared in wonderment.

"What happened? Why are you on the battlefield?" Asked Casey in amazement.

They sat together in the ER waiting on the doctor. Four stitches and an x-ray later they were ready to sign out. The nurse motioned them to follow her and Casey signed the papers to kick in her insurance.

Benj watched her from the corner of her eye as they headed home. Casey sat with her head hung in perfect silence.

"Casey?" Benj said quietly. "Yep." Casey answered. Benj shrugged and threw up her hands in a questioning motion. "What the hell?" She finally asked.

"I can't even begin to tell you." Casey looked at Benj tears welling in her soon to be black eyes.

"Benj I need to ask you the same question. What the hell! I have no idea what happened. We were driving along and I smelled the smoke! That was all I remember...smelling the smoke." Casey looked so miserable

Benj couldn't stand much more.

"What smoke? What smoke Case?" Benj asked as they drove into the driveway. "What the hell smoke did you smell on this beautiful day in the middle of summer in podunk Oklahoma?"

"I smelled smoke and I looked on that ridge and the boys were just coming into view and I knew, I knew what was coming..I knew what was happening...."

"So you jumped your ass out of a moving truck?" shouted Benj. Casey hung her head tears staining the front of her t-shirt.

"I guess I did, yeah."

"Come on Casey. Lets get in the house and relax a bit. We need to get a bag a frozen peas on that face of yours. Honest to God did you have to do a direct face plant right out of the friggin' truck? I almost had a breakdown seeing you sprawled and bleeding on the gravel! Holy shit Case!" Benj gently took Casey's arm and helped her out of the passenger seat.

"I'm not crippled you know." Casey mumbled.

"No, your just crazy. Crazy as a bowl of bedbugs. Crazy as a hatter on crack. Crazy as a snake on hot asphalt." Casey started to smile. "It hurts to smile." She complained to Benj. "Oh good!" said Benj unlocking the door and holding it open. "Then this good dope they gave you at the hospital will come in handy!"

Casey put down the hand mirror and fell back against the sofa.

"Gonna leave a scar isn't it?" She glanced at Benj standing in the kitchen. "It will add character to your big, white face. Lord knows that big ole' Irish mug a yours could use some character." Benj brought two glasses of Pepsi in and looked thoughtfully at the bruised and broken face of her friend.

"Okay, spill." She demanded.

Chapter 23

Benj woke to the sound of Casey calling in sick to work.

"Yeah, I had a little accident. No, no, I'm just fine, just need a day to get my feet back under me is all. Oh no, I'll be back tomorrow don't you worry about that! Okay, thanks so much…I'll make up the time I promise." Benj picked up a piece of buttered toast and gave her friend a long hard look.

"You look like shit." She said chewing nosily.

"Ya think?" replied Casey.

"Sorta like the Phantom Of The Opera, huh?" She smiled lopsidedly.

"Funny thing is I slept straight through the night! No spooks, no bumps in the night, no nothin'. Pretty cool huh?" Casey grinned crooked and painful, kicking Benj under the table. "You were stoned to the tits. You were wasted off your ass. That's what good pharmaceuticals will do for you." Benj kicked back and cocked her head.

"Maybe that's the answer, we have to turn you into a dope fiend and then your goofy little "gift" will behave." Casey laughed.

"Dope fiend? When was the last time anyone use the term 'dope fiend'. You'd be the laughing stock of all the meth heads everywhere if that got out." Casey joked.

The girls leaned back against the worn old sofa and sighed in unison.

"I've got to go back." said Casey looking sideways at her friend.

"Yeah, I know that. I just wish you weren't so banged up before we go there." Benj sighed in resignation.

"When do you want to go?" Benj asked.

"I guess now's as good a time as any don't you think?" Benj looked away running her hand thru her short hair.

"Suppose."

The day was one of those overcast and hot ones that can only be described if you've been there. Soft and sultry and make your ears ring humid.

"I'm bringing water." Benj announced. Casey stood in the driveway and pointed across the highway.

"It's right there Benj! I mean right there! You can see our tire tracks from yesterday in the damn gravel! We will not be visiting the Sahara!"

"Yeah well let me tell you a thing or

two Miss Smarty Pants, I'm damn glad I had a bottle of water in my hand yesterday when you were bleedin' all up and down the pavement!" Benj said with conviction.

"It's gravel."

"What?"

"It's gravel! There is no pavement!"

"Oh for Gods sake! Get in the truck!" Benj hollered grabbing a bottle of water and tossing it in beside her. Benj started the old engine and glanced over at Casey.

"Put your seat belt on. I don't want you lungin' out the door again."

Casey fastened the belt over her shoulder without a peep.

Casey smelled the smoke before they even rolled up on the ridge of the hill. She dug her fingernails into the worn cover of the passenger seat.

"You okay?" asked Benj flashing Casey a worried look.

"Yep, fine." Casey nodded looking more then a little unsure. "Benj, I can smell the smoke already." Benj glanced at her friend.

"Do you want me to pull over?" Casey shook her head and stared straight ahead.

"Just stay with me Benj. Okay?" Benj laid her hand on Casey's clenched hand.

"Always" she muttered. "No matter how nuts this gets."

Benj drove slowly over the bridge, ancient and crumbling. Repair after repair had kept this structure hangin' but it didn't look like it could take a lot more.

"Benj pull over!" Casey whispered.

"Right here?" Benj asked.

"Yeah." Casey nodded. "Come with

me."

"Really? You want me to come to the battlefield?" Benj looked shocked.

"Yeah."

They walked slowly up the hill together but somehow out of time, out of sync. Casey smelled wood smoke and green grass and unwashed men. Benj smelled the lovely smell of blue stem waving around them. The humming of bugs and humidity spinning circles around there heads. At the crest of the hill Casey sat down. She watched as the men far to young to be soldiers but soldiers all the same, laughed and goofed and swatted each other in play. Some sat in front of tents cleaning rifles or reading. Some held paper in there laps writing letters to loved ones and sealing envelopes.

Some cooked meals on small fires

with black pots dangling above.

Casey watched the peaceful scene knowing far to well what was to come. She felt a smile cross her face as she spotted the two young boys sitting at the fringe of the activity practicing drums on tree stumps.

A man she recognized stepped from one of the tents. He was stooped and tired, his uniform dirty and torn. She watched as he moved from man to man talking and placing his hand on the weary shoulders of each. Suddenly he turned and looked directly at Casey. His worn and bearded face looked relieved somehow as he deftly tipped his battered hat toward her.

"Benj? Benj you there?" Casey said not moving a muscle.

"You know I am." Benj said in almost a whisper. "Do you see anything?"

"I do." Casey grabbed Benj's hand and held on tight.

"I see everything."

Chapter 24

    Benj sat stock still as Casey squeezed and released her hand. She didn't know what was going on over there in Casey's world but she knew it was something unforgettable. Every now and again Casey would squeeze her hand in a death grip then slowly let go. Casey's hand would go from warm and inviting to cold and sweaty in a matter of seconds. Benj held tight.

    Benj felt a change in the air around them and a distant roll of thunder made her sit up and take notice. Coming up from the west, dark clouds were gathering in the almost unbreathable humidity. The wind picked up slightly blowing the tall blue stem against them in sharp little arrows.

"Casey! Casey!" Benj whispered. "Weather comin'."

Casey watched as the two drummer boys scurried over to the Officer. They saluted awkwardly and pointed toward the bubbling little creek. It was hot, Casey knew what they wanted. They were dirty and sweaty and covered with grime and smoke and who knew what else.

"Boys just wanna have fun." Casey whispered to herself.

"What?" Benj said as she saw Casey's lips smile slightly and move.

"What boy's wanna have fun? I hope your not seein' a Cindi Lauper video in that head of yours cause we could be doing that at home!" Benj looked up at the darkening sky so huge above them. Sitting out in the open on top of a ridge made it all seem that much more foreboding. Benj squirmed slightly and cradled Casey's hand.

"You had better wrap this up quick my friend....we got weather!"Suddenly a crack of thunder made Benj jump straight in the air and the wind blew hard against her face.

Casey heard the first round of cannon fire and the ground shook under her. She watched as the young soldiers grabbed hats and guns and dropped to the ground. Casey turned her head toward the creek, the creek that the two boys had just run toward! She watched as the Officer went from man to man stuffing the letters they were writing in his vest and making sure they were unharmed and armed. Bent at the waist he ran to the supply wagon and threw back the canvas flap.

Inside Casey could see stacked pots and pans, food and all the rest of the things a company of soldiers would need. The Officer reached inside a wooden box, a steamer trunk, with a squared off top, and somehow a shallow drawer slid out of the front. He gently placed the letters his men had written to their loved ones inside the drawer and slammed it shut. The gunfire started in earnest then and Casey squinted her eyes against the reality of the battle.

Cannons boomed all around her and the sky grew dark with smoke and screams of the dying. Casey watched in horror as one by one the men she had watched moments before, men so alive and filled with laughter and comradeship fell to their deaths. Casey squeezed so hard on Benj's hand she thought she may break it.

Benj lowered her face to her chest as the deluge broke around her. Thunder cracked and the sky turned to midnight. She lowered herself closer to the ground in hopes it might protect her and Casey. She held Casey's hand so tight she could barely feel the squeezing that was happening there. "Casey!" Benj shouted. "We have to go!"

Casey sat as still as death as the storm passed above them. Tears dribbled down her chin as the last moans and cries disappeared into the Oklahoma soil. She watched as marauders, killers, murders...murders just as young, just as scared, just as dirty and skinny as the dead that lay around them, came thru the underbrush. They raided the wagons for food and supplies. They dumped what they thought was useless in and around the creek. They took the shoes from the dead and the jacket from the Officer. They hung there heads and tears made dirty rivers down there young faces. They dragged there rifles thru the mud soaked creek bed not caring anymore. They stared into the faces of the boys they robbed of there short lives. The ones so like themselves.

Suddenly the wind blew and the sky opened. Rain fell over Benj and Casey like a soaking shroud. Benj jumped to her feet ready to carry Casey out if she had to! But she didn't, Casey looked up at her, tears blending with the pouring rain on her face.

"What the hell Benj! Let go!" Casey jumped to her feet and ran toward the truck with Benj close behind.

As they ducked into the protection of the bouncing, swaying windblown truck Benj pushed the soaking hair off of her forehead.

"You okay Case?" She looked suspiciously toward her dripping friend.

"Yeah." Casey scrunched her face and wiped a stray drip from her chin. "I think I might be more then okay Benj, Honest to God." Casey slumped down low in the seat and laid her head back. "Man, I'm so tired though, so friggin' tired."

Chapter 25

"What the heck is wrong with her anyway? Is she dyin'?

Casey heard whispers coming from over her head.

"I'm not dying." She mumbled slowly. "I'm tired."

"I think she's just tired." Casey heard the voice again wafting just above face.

"She's been asleep for two days for Christs sake!" Casey smiled to herself as she heard the frustration oozing out of Benj's voice.

"Why isn't she peein' herself or anything? It's like she's in a friggin' coma! I don't like it one bit."

Casey smiled to again tho the concept of peeing was becoming a little more then an idea. Casey felt someone pick up her hand and hold it for a minute or two.

"She's just fine." The unknown voice floated through her mind.

"Good to know." Casey thought smiling to herself once again.

"I have to pee!" Casey's voice sounded gravely and her mouth tasted like a three day old sock was living there, but that she made heard.

"Why did you have to mention peeing Benj, threw me all off." Casey opened one eye in a tiny slit and turned it toward the voices. Benj stood next to one of the nurses from her office, both with their eyes shocked and bulging at her sudden return to the land of the living.

"Help me!"

"I need a bath." Casey mumbled.

"Yes you do." Benj replied helping

Casey get her footing.

"My teeth are growing things."

"Yes, I'm sure they are." Both girls chuckled as Benj plopped Casey on the toilet.

"I'm running you a bath." Benj announced.

"Oh good! Man, I could use a good cup a coffee that's for sure." Casey mumbled. "And I have no idea what's going on with my hair!"

"It'll wash!" Benj shouted heading toward the kitchen.

"Do you remember anything after the storm? Do you remember coming in the house? Do you remember getting home from out on the battlefield?" Benj poured a cup of strong coffee for both of them as she hit Casey with questions.

We came running in the door and you said you had to go to bed! And you did! Just like that...not to be heard from again for two full days! You scared the bejeebers straight out of me with that crap Casey! Finally I had to have Darleen from your office come look in on you! Damn Case!

"I was so tired Benj." Casey picked at a piece of frayed tablecloth. Sometimes I could hear you talking and I tried to let you know I was okay. That was some kind of sleepin' experience I'm tellin' you." Casey sipped at the coffee, made a face and gave Benj the stink eye.

"This is terrible coffee Benj, just sayin'."

"Yeah, yeah it's always terrible unless you make it. I know, I know. So? Now that your back from the dead spill it! Benj plopped down in the old wooden kitchen chair and wrapped her fingers around the over sized cup in front of her.

"You've got lots of splainin' to do Lucy!"

"I'm not sure I can explain much Benj, honestly I'm not. But, one thing I do know is we have to get a hold of Sheriff Elwood soon enough!" Casey turned her dark rimmed eyes toward Benj. "Wanna go now?" Benj shook her head and slapped her open palm on the table. "No! Honestly no! You look like death on it's last go around and you need to rest!" Benj took a long, long breath and stared at her friend. "If you'll take it easy tonight we'll both take a ride to town tomorrow. But please indulge me and take this evening. I'll run to town and get some burgers from the Dairy Queen and we can curl up and watch a good movie. Enough dead people for today...Enough dead people for ever if you ask me!" Benj dropped her tired head to her hand. "One quiet evening, that's all I ask Case, please, just one!"

Casey smiled and touched her friends arm. "Deal! I doubt I could make it past the porch without dropin' in a faint anyway."

"Yoohoo!" The strange voice rattled through the old house like a warm wind. "Who's that?" Casey asked flipping a soft, puffy pancake. "You expectin' anyone?" She asked Benj.

"I am!" Said Casey's partner in crime with a smug look on her freshly scrubbed face. The evenings relaxation had done the world of good for both of them and Casey was back on duty at the front of the waiting stove. Coffee was brewing and bacon was sizzling for the makings of a dream breakfast!

"Oh my Heaven's! I've been delivered to some sort of land of glory!" Sheriff Elwood followed his nose straight to the cozy kitchen and lingered over the coffeepot. "Do you think you could spare a cup a this nectar of the Gods this mornin' Casey?"

"Why you sit right down there Sheriff your just the man I've been wanting to talk to." Casey filled a big ole' mug with fresh coffee and sat it in front of the officer. "I've got plenty of bacon and pancakes here if your hungry Sheriff, how's that sound?"

"You don't have to pull my leg one bit Casey! Your cookin' is enough to get me anywhere this early in the mornin'. The call from Benj was a tip off though. What exactly can I do for you ladies?" Casey gave Benj the once over but Benj just shrugged. "I figured if the Sheriff was in the area he might enjoy a good breakfast and we wouldn't have to drag your semi-sick self to town today. Made sense to me!" Benj sipped her coffee and gave Casey an all knowing grin.

Sheriff Elwood shoved a forkful of sweet, puffy goodness in his mouth. "Works for me!" He mumbled around the avalanche of food.

Casey slid her chair out and plopped herself across from the chewing officer. "Elwood, did you send that box that dead boy was in off to Oklahoma City yet?" Casey asked looking earnestly over her steaming mug. "I'm just wonderin' if there's any news." Casey asked.

"Well, the wheels of the law move a little slow here in Hughes County now Casey." The Officer sipped his cooling coffee.

"We've had a lot of thing's goin' on with the new High School and the hot dog fundraiser over't the Pentecostal Holiness. All that and the pie auction and this town's been a hoppin' place for the last week or so!" The Sheriff mopped his face with a folded napkin and cleared his throat looking sheepishly at Casey.

"Where's it at then?" Casey asked.

"Well, it's sittin' over't the Library in the capable hands of Miss Constance. Best place for it to be, till we can get it packed up and ready to travel."

A huge smile spread across Casey's face as she shoved a crispy piece of bacon in her waiting mouth.

Chapter 26

"But Miss Constance, we really need to see it." Casey found herself begging her good friend and serious Librarian. "Please Miss Constance!" Casey implored.

"Casey, Honey I know very well your not gonna go hurtin' that piece of history. I, better then anyone know how you feel about that sort of thing. I just don't want you fallin' into one of your fits when the building is filled with all sorts of children and everybody else in this town can just roll on up in here. Your just gonna have to wait till I shut the doors on the day or come on back at the weekend! Now I won't hear a word a back talk about that!" Miss Constance turned her back on the earnest Casey and

Benj to check a video out for woman with a baby strapped to her chest.

"I cain't have that sort of thing anymore!" Miss Constance whispered over her shoulder.

"Though I am dying to find out exactly what's got you two so riled!" Miss Constance smiled at the woman and clucked the baby under it's chin.

"That movie's due back tomorrow. You have a lovely evening now Carol Ann and say hi to your Mama will ya?"

Casey slid down into a waiting chair and dropped her head in her hands.

"Wanna go to the Dairy Queen and get a Blizzard while we wait?" Benj asked. Casey lifted her head and gazed at her friend.

"You buyin'?" She asked smiling.

"Well, I've got a taste for one of those Butterfinger things so I guess I am. You followin'?

"I guess I am." answered Casey.

"Case?" Benj laid her head back and squinted at the warm Oklahoma sun.

"You think your gonna go into another one of your fits? I mean this last one was a doozy and I'm not sure any of us are ready for another like that." Benj looked worried and shifted her gaze toward her friend.

"I honestly don't know. I have some sort of feeling that it may not happen this time. I think things are wrappin' up I might get a break." Casey propped her feet up against a neighboring picnic table. "I don't think I could take another bout like we just had, that's for sure!"

"I'm gonna call Elwood and see if he

wants to meet us over't the Library when it closes. I'd rather be safe then sorry."

The sun was peekin' around the trees casting beautiful shadows before Miss Constance was able to shush the last client out of the Library. Silence fell around the place like a gentle shroud. The girls walked reverently through the dusky aisles taking note of the ancient titles. Since the Library had opened as a free video outlet and the town video store had closed, the old books got very little attention. Casey ran her finger over the dust that lay around the old leather bound volumes.

"It's all gonna be lost one day. Just like Jules Vern predicted. All these books will crumble to dust when someone touches them.

"Well, aren't you a little ray of sunshine." Benj replied. Casey smiled and let her hand run over the muted colors of the bindings.

"Tell me it's not true." She mumbled.

Suddenly Casey stopped dead in her tracks! Benj followed her eyes to the two large boxes shoved under a table to the very back of the building.

"They're still here!" Casey gasped.

"Of course they are Honey! Where else would they go? After all the mystery was solved we brought them right back where they belonged." Miss Constance lightly held Casey's arm.

"Don't worry Casey, that is all water under the bridge now. Lawnwood is solved and put to rest. You have nothing else to fear from those boxes now Honey. They are there for the curious and the researchers. Your part is over. Come on Sweetie, there's another adventure for you to look into." Miss Constance held tightly to Casey's arm and steered her further back in the unused portion of the elderly building. As Casey approached the metal strapped wooden box it seemed to glow in the dim light. Casey could feel the years the box had existed. So many lives it had touched or witnessed in one way or the next. Casey's mind fluttered and reeled as she stood staring at the object. Such a simple thing, such day to day item yet so much life and love had passed through and over this scarred old trunk. Life lost, life won. Casey glanced at Benj.

"You okay?" Casey barely heard the words her friend uttered. In her mind the sun shined on a beautiful day.

Boys having fun in the creek. Young men relaxing and enjoying a moment of rest.

"No! No!" Casey shook her head and cleared the images. "I can't! I can't go there!" She looked desperately at Benj digging her fingernails into the soft part of Benj's arm.

"You wanna go?" Benj asked. "You wanna leave? We don't have to do this Casey! We can walk right out of here now and never come back. Honest to God Case! No one would blame you."

Casey's mind flipped to a young girl scared and hurting, running as fast as she could to get away. Muffled laughter coming from the end of a long, long hallway, coming from this box, this box! Casey wanted to run! She wanted to puke or spit or hit someone. In her fury she walked to the box and opened it. With one finger she tripped a secret trigger long hidden. A simple device no one realized was there. All around her the air was filled with confetti. Pieces of paper flew and ebbed around her head and face. The palpable smell of wood smoke rimmed the room. Ribbons and pieces of cloth spun around and tumbled to the floor at her feet.

"What the hell?" Casey heard Benj exclaim. "What is all this?" Casey turned to Benj.

"It's the answer." Casey smiled slightly as she slumped to the ground among the bits of yellowed letters written well over a hundred years ago. Bits of paper that told of a war between families and states and the horror of it all. Ribbons earned on the battlefields of that war that no one had time to sew on raggedy uniforms.

Photos of pretty girls sitting stoically waiting for there boys to return. These boys. These young men fallen and forgotten in the mud and anger of an Oklahoma creek bed. These young men killed and put aside by history and another group of young men just as battered and forgotten. It was all there. A story never told. A story lost but now found.

Casey closed her eyes and let the enormity wash over her. Tears crawled down her face as she watched a face so beaten and tired. A face no history book held in it's binding. She watched as that face turned and walked away with a single tip of a sweat brimmed hat. It was finished now. Casey passed out cold.

Chapter 27

The phone jangled in Casey's scrub pocket. She slid into the seat of her Chevy Truck before she tapped the button to answer it.

"Hey! How was your flight? You get home okay? Did you stock up on tax free booze at O'Hare?" Casey laughed into the phone and rolled down the window to the hot breeze streaming through her truck.

"I'm great! Got home fine and dandy. Nothing is as exciting as a vacation in Weirdville though I must admit." Benj replied.

"Oh I know! Now your gonna have to go back to ploppin' in front of that computer all day with no rattlin' chains or spooks hangin' out overhead! Whatever will you do?" Casey asked in a clear mocking voice.

"Not sure, but I'm willing to try that's for certain. You don't have any wraiths or bumps in the night goin' on anymore do you?" Benj asked with just the slightest concern edging her voice.

"Not a thing. Sleepin' like a newborn these days. O' course it's hotter'n Hades around here now. You went home just in time..we are steamin' and about cooked!" Casey laughed and stuck her head out to the very slight breeze. "Honestly Benj, all is well. The spooks are leavin' me alone, hopefully forever this time. People are startin' to talk!" Casey smiled in the bright sunlight.

"I'm so glad so many families were able to find peace in those letters from long lost loved ones. That had to be so cool for them. To suddenly know that some Great Uncle or Great Grandfather fought in a battle out in the middle of nowhere. One of the last battles of the Civil War. Kinda weird to get a letter someone wrote over a hundred years ago don't you think?"

"I do!" But all that stuff answered a lot of questions for a lot of people."

"And put some to rest. Don't forget about that."

"That I can't forget!"

"Casey don't be goofy, you know people always gonna talk. That's what they do in small towns. It's the National pastime around there. Don't kid yourself Sweetie, they got your number! And, with all that weird as hell stuff goin' on don't think your not the subject of every dinner conversation."

"Oh I'm countin' on it! Keeps the

riff-raff away! Okay Kiddo, I've gotta get to work. Don't forget about me way out here in the middle of nowhere will ya?" Casey grinned but a moment of sadness passed over her. She missed having Benj around. Even if it was just to share a meal in the evenings or laugh at a good movie. Her friend was the best company she could think of.

"Okay Girly, stay out of trouble and please, please don't touch anything! Love you! See you next trip down!"

Casey listened for a long time to the dial tone buzzing in her ear. Then her thoughts turned to Miss Ellie and the adventure they were about to have. She put the phone back in her purse and started the big truck toward her elderly friends home. Casey watched the dust rise under the tires as she rolled along. "Need rain!" She said to no-one, though she knew in her heart a world of people could hear her musings. Casey started to laugh and swiped her hand around the cab of her truck..."Come on y'all! We have live people to visit!"

Miss Ellie was all smiles when Casey walked in.

"What's up with you? You swallow the canary?" Casey joked pouring herself a cup of good coffee.

"Nope, just waitin' on yer visit! I thought you might be getting' a bit lonely since your buddy took back off for the big city." Miss Ellie said beaming at Casey.

"I am a bit but you know I'm a hermit at heart so things will settle down back to normal here soon enough." Casey stirred her coffee and took a tentative sip. "Ahhhhh! Good coffee!" She smiled.

"How you feelin' about all this hot weather we're havin'?" Miss Ellie said gazing out the window.

"I'm about sick to death of it and it's just now startin' up!" Casey watched the ripples of heat rising' off the early morning asphalt. "What are we gonna do today anyway? You need your bed made up today?" Casey leaned back and enjoyed her good cup of coffee.

"Yeah, you can make up the bed but

what I'd really like is for you to run to the restaurant and get us a mess of that good fish there cookin' over there. I've had such a taste lately." Miss Ellie wiped her mouth and looked hungry.

"Ha!" Casey hooted. "That is exactly what my job description says! Run get fried fish once the catfish start runnin'! It's right there in the handbook." Miss Ellie reached out and slapped Casey's hand.

"Don't be a smart-ass, I'll share."

"You got yourself a deal in that case." Casey laughed.

"You gonna go to the beauty shop tomorrow and get your hair done?" Casey hollered from the bedroom.

"A course I am, you don't want me runnin' around this town lookin' like a wild woman do you?" Miss Ellie hollered back. "You better get a move on over't the restaurant before they sell out a that fish. I'm just waterin' at the mouth over that stuff these days. One good thing you have to say about summer and that's the catfish is tasty!"

"They aren't gonna sell out at ten in the morning but I'll scoot over there now if you want me to. Are we gonna wait till noon to eat it?"

"No we're gonna eat it when you get back here! Now git!" Miss Ellie handed some money to Casey and motioned her out the door.

"So we are having catfish for breakfast then?" Casey laughed while swinging around the corner.

"I had my breakfast at six AM! Don't know what you been doin' all day but my belly is already actin' up! Git!"

Casey dipped the last surviving piece of fresh catfish in tarter sauce and popped it in her mouth.

"I have to admit that was worth the trip." Casey sat back in the tall kitchen chair.

"Oh my goodness, now I need to go down for a nap!" Miss Ellie chuckled.

"You can't. Your beds not made." Casey teased. Casey gathered there lunch dishes and ran some water in the kitchen sink. She knew Miss Ellie would be shifting around her dentures a bit after the meal and decided to leave her some privacy for that activity. Casey scrubbed down the plates and rinsed them slowly in the warm water.

"Miss Ellie?" Casey asked with her back turned.

"What Honey." Miss Ellie replied.

"Did you know Clyde Ray Tummel would die in that box up on the third floor?"

Casey could feel the air and all the fight go out of her friend and when she turned around she swore her face was ten years older.

"No Honey, I never, ever knew what happened to him after that day he hurt me." Miss Ellie hung her head. "I knew if anyone found out what happened up there my reputation would be ruined. You know Casey, I knew somehow you knew about all this. I knew someday it would come up. I just didn't know when.

Casey sat down next to her good friend and took her hand.

"I saw right away once I was up there. I didn't know how to bring it up though."

"Girls were always to blame back then Casey. If word got out my life in this town would have been ruined."

"He raped you." Casey said. "That

wasn't your fault."

"It was a different time Honey. It was the last day of school and he said some terrible things to me. Called me awful names and then he, did what he did." Miss Ellie wiped a tear off of her soft face.

"When it was over he was laughing at me. I was upset and crying. I shoved him and he fell into that steamer trunk. I slammed the lid down and ran like heck. It was all I could think to do!"

"I can't blame you for that. I'd have done the same." Casey handed her friend a tissue and squeezed her hand.

"I knew he was missing, I knew people were lookin' for him. I told myself he did run off with the circus and he'd be back round the next season. But, he never came back, and I never went back up to that third floor again!" Miss Ellie wiped her nose and looked straight in Casey's eyes. "You gonna tattle on me?"

Casey shook her head and tightened her grip on the old woman's hand.

"Never, I promise."

Made in the USA
Columbia, SC
25 September 2019